# JACKIE MANTHORNE

# WITHOUT WINGS

WITHDRAWN

D1592813

gynergy books

COPYRIGHT © JACKIE MANTHORNE, 1993

All rights reserved. No part of this book may be reproduced
or transmitted in any form or by any means without permission of the
publisher, except by a reviewer, who may quote brief passages in a
review.

COVER ILLUSTRATION: Janet Riopelle
PRINTED AND BOUND IN CANADA BY: Webcom

*gynergy books acknowledges the generous support
of the Canada Council.*

PUBLISHED BY:
gynergy books
P.O. Box 2023
Charlottetown, P.E.I.
Canada  C1A 7N7


DISTRIBUTORS:
Canada: General Publishing
United States: Inland Book Company
United Kingdom: Turnaround Distribution


CANADIAN CATALOGUING IN PUBLICATION DATA
Manthorne, Jackie, 1946-

Without wings
ISBN 0-921881-29-0

I. Title.

PS8576.A568W57 1993   C813'.54   C93-098654-7
PR9199.3.M36W57 1993

PR
9199.3
·M3494
W58
1993

52895

# Contents

1   Rude Awakening

13   Pool Shock

21   Charades

29   Heartache

36   A Night To Remember

48   Change of Heart

55   No More Words

64   Taking Liberties

72   Dirty Words

82   The Wrong Menu

88   Crossroads

98   Double Trouble

107   Muted Memories

114   Silent Night

121   Spilled Beer

127   Free To Love

134   Soft Touch

142   Four O'clock and All's Well

152   Indecision

157   A Night On the Town

165   Friendship

# Rude Awakening

The minute Oats opened the door to l'Entr'acte, her senses were assailed by the thick beat of the music, the pungent fumes of beer, the fog of cigarette smoke and the acrid odour of sweat blended with several varieties of cheap perfume. She felt like an ex-con furtively breaking parole, but being alone in the bar wasn't such a sin. It was harmless, really. And it was certainly better than sitting at home on a Friday night waiting for something to happen, for her lover Melba to call or for a friend to drop by for a couple of beers and a game or two of poker. Waiting made her feel claustrophobic; she needed action, even other people's. She never felt this way when Melba was home, but Melba was in Toronto for the weekend, visiting her younger sister, who was probably giving birth to her first child right this very minute.

Oats had tried to control her restlessness, stopping at the corner store on the way home from work to pick up a six-pack of beer and a jumbo bag of potato chips, both of the "lite" variety to ease her guilty conscience about the growing spare tire around her middle and the spreading behind she couldn't see but knew was there. But chips and beer mixed with solitude upset her psyche as well as her stomach, so she made a deal with herself: she would drop by l'Entr'acte for one beer. That was all. Just one innocent little beer and some innocuous chit-chat, and then she would turn around and go right back home and watch a couple of late-night TV shows until she got tired enough to fall sleep.

Oats checked her leather jacket and walked warily into the bar, already on her best behaviour. There would be no fooling around. No flirting. No cruising. Nothing she could be reproached for. But despite her best intentions, the sight of all those women besotted her, and she was swiftly overcome by a heady sense of adventure. It was a dangerous feeling, and she knew it. She tended to fall hard and fast for a pretty face, a promising curve of the breast, a shapely leg. Sometimes even a come-hither glint in the eye was enough to push her over the edge. She knew she shouldn't expose herself to danger, but being Oats, she sat down on a bar stool and did what she always did: smiled at the bartender, ordered a beer, lit a cigarette and instinctively scanned the crowd of women clustered around the bar, looking for somebody who was looking for somebody.

"Your predatory instincts are showing," Melba had quipped one evening as she, Oats and a group of their friends walked into l'Entr'acte, Oats strutting like she owned the place. Everybody had laughed, even Oats, although Melba's offhand comment had shamed her. She knew that she had a risqué, perhaps even unsavoury reputation; after all, she had made cruising women a second career, and she had never bothered to be secretive about it. Actually, she had rather gloried in it. But Melba made it sound cheap, dirty, something to be hidden away behind closed doors. Was it? Oats didn't know. She didn't think so; after all, it felt good, and wasn't that what life was all about?

Oats didn't know why Melba loved her, but then, neither did anyone else. Everybody said they were emotionally incompatible. Melba didn't play games. She said what she meant, and always meant what she said. She fell in love and stayed in love for an unimaginably long time. She believed in working on a relationship. As for the pre-Melba Oats, she rarely told the truth, or at least not the whole truth. The words which left her mouth were intended to charm, to beguile, to seduce. Love was mentioned when it was convenient, forgotten when it wasn't. Which was often, since variety was more important to her than stability. Fidelity was a bore, jealousy a plague, monogamy worse than death. She was fearless in pursuit, careless in escape. She hurt women in the process, but most of the time she was too busy to notice.

Oats had been faithful to Melba for six months. She hadn't even felt like cheating. That was unusual, and sometimes, when she stopped long enough to think about it, it frightened her. Where was the lifelong restlessness which gripped her with great regularity shortly after she professed fervent adoration and eternal devotion? What had happened to her need to control every facet of her life? Would her rambling nature reassert itself, and if so, when? Would she ever wake up with the old familiar feeling that everything was as stale as day-old toast and it was time to move on?

Not that Melba cramped her style; on the contrary, Oats loved her very much. The sex was great. She had even grown accustomed to having somebody around all the time. There was nothing missing, although sometimes she felt a vague nostalgia which made her sad. She pined for the sexual tension and the suspense of cruising; experience had taught her that success was the best release, nearly always more important than the sex which followed. Success translated into power, which reverberated along her nervous system like a taut wire vibrating in the wind. The urge to cruise was in her blood and always had been. Without this excitement, her body felt drained, lacking in energy. At times she didn't know what to do with herself. Not that Melba wasn't enough, although Oats often wondered about her own capacity to respond to this kind of love. Could she be serious forever? Honest all the time? Happy day-in, day-out, without constant adulation? But these were difficult questions, and she didn't try very hard to answer them. It was easier to drift with the tide and let the days and nights go by without questioning whether she was capable of swimming in such deep waters.

Oats raised her eyes from the bar and looked at the woman sitting across from her. She had noticed her seconds after sitting down, but then, who wouldn't have? Not that she had an "I am available" sign plastered across her forehead, but she might as well have had. The signals were obvious and strong. Her clothes, her posture, the expression on her face and the message in her eyes announced to anybody who wanted to know that she was ready. Ready and waiting. Oats stared; the woman stared back. Openly. And with interest.

This was possible, Oats thought. But it was also impossible. And wrong. She had no right to pursue it. She was there for a beer, to escape the vapid solitude of her apartment, nothing more, nothing less. So she took a sip of the evening's raison d'etre and made an effort. She was committed to somebody else. She had promised to be faithful, and all that nonsense. No, wait, it wasn't nonsense: she was in love with a wonderful woman, and she shouldn't even be *looking*, much less *thinking* about you-know-what.

So what if the woman in question was attractive, the answer to any hungry dyke's weekend prayers? So what if she was obviously looking for somebody, patiently waiting to be cruised? No matter how hard you tried or how many times you came, in the final analysis, it was all transitory. Come morning, the pale winter sun would eventually rise and remind you that the earth hadn't moved in a permanent way (if it had even moved at all, which was by no means assured just because you were both horny to begin with). And life would go on in spite of all those wonderful orgasms. Time itself wasn't going to stop for you; in reality, it wasn't even going to notice whether you were having a good time or not. The second hand was just going to keep turning with relentless regularity while you were otherwise preoccupied, making you one day older with not much to show for it except a slight hangover and sore muscles. But with her reputation as a lady-killer on the prowl freshly resurrected in her mind, Oats wasn't thinking about that; she was too busy puffing up her image as a sophisticated butch, intent on making first impressions count.

But why? Who did she think she was, Casanova? Oats stopped making eye contact, finished her beer and resolved to resist temptation. If an old dog could learn new tricks, so could a middle-aged dyke. Yeah, and the cow jumped over the moon and came down alive and kicking without benefit of wings or a parachute, she thought sourly. Sex wasn't everything, or so some people claimed. Unfortunately, Oats didn't believe them. She hated being alone on the weekend, even though she knew she wasn't really alone, as in single, lonely, horny, hungry for company, for a little companionship, for some tender loving or even some mindless, funky sex for a couple of hours in the back seat of a car or between messy sheets in a stranger's bed. Whatever. And wherever. But she wasn't desperate; her lover was temporarily out of town, not gone forever.

Where was Melba when she needed her? And for that matter, where were all her friends? Just because it was winter and the indifferent, grey sky was about to dump a couple tons of snow on Montreal and the temperature was nearly low enough to freeze lust in its tracks didn't give her friends the right to stay home. Or temporarily escape the mid-winter blahs by hopping a plane to Florida to mingle on the hot, sandy beach with most of the rest of the population of Montreal. Not even one of her ex-lovers was there to partake in a little harmless flirtation, to distract her from the unspoken but clearly implied invitation from the stranger across the bar, to indulge in a little Friday night hanky-panky.

Oats sighed, ordered another beer, lit a cigarette, and hunkered down to some diversionary drinking. She knew she should leave, but she couldn't unglue herself from the bar stool. On the other hand, why should she be scared off? After all, this bar was as much her territory as anybody else's. She would simply ignore the other woman. That way she wouldn't be tempted. After this beer she would go home and take a cold shower to wash the bar from her skin. Or go for a long walk in the snow until her imagination froze and she was too cold to feel horny. If that was the way to a virtuous life, so be it. She sighed yet again, frustrated; she really didn't want to resist temptation. And Melba was in Toronto, which was probably a message from some higher power that this was meant to be. Then too, the most significant message-bearer of all was sitting right across from Oats, a knowing smile on her face. And Oats, who really did love Melba, still wanted that smiling woman something fierce, and before she knew it, she was rashly crossing the great divide between thought and action, between temptation and giving into it. Say what you will, but sinning in her mind was never enough for Oats.

"Sue Dobbs." She extended her hand, curling it suggestively, as if her fingers were about to reach out and touch something intimate. "Oats."

"Frédérique." She took Oats' outstretched hand and her skin was so soft that Oats wondered for a fleeting second if they had really touched. But it didn't matter. Oats was infatuated, and no little bit in lust.

"Come dance with me," Oats said huskily. There wouldn't be any harm in having a dance or two, she rationalized. After all, she had danced with lots of women since she met Melba, and nothing untoward had happened. Perhaps she had been turned on now and then in spite of her best intentions, but there was nothing wrong with that. Especially since she hadn't mentioned it to anyone, not even Melba. Especially not Melba.

"Dance?" Frédérique mused, her pronunciation French. Oats watched Frédérique run her tongue over her lips and imagined doing the same thing herself.

"Yes, dance," Oats replied, laughing gruffly as she rose and gently pulled Frédérique to her feet, led her to the dance floor and took her in her arms, closing her eyes so tight that they flashed red when Frédérique leaned against her. The friction of their moving bodies was electrifying, and Oats' uncertainty dissolved as effortlessly as sugar in a hot cup of coffee. She couldn't possibly turn back now.

Oats slid her hands up and down Frédérique's back in time to the music. "Come home with me."

"Mais oui," Frédérique replied at once. Oats saw the heat bubble up in Frédérique's eyes and knew it was mirrored in her own. This woman was already primed, and so was she. It was going to be wonderful, like the first taste of a frosty, celebratory beer after you hit a home run and maintained a torrid, show-off pace around the bases on a hot, steamy, mid-summer afternoon. And it had been such a long, long time …

Damn! Wasn't that Kate pushing toward them through the crowd? Sure it was. Double-damn! She was going to get caught. She had already seen a couple of people she knew, including that cute little student Jo and her punk girlfriend, but they didn't matter; they were acquaintances, not good friends. They wouldn't make trouble, not like Kate was going to.

"Well, well, well. Imagine meeting you here," Kate said.

"Yeah," Oats drawled, her mouth dry. Frédérique was hanging possessively on her arm; Oats wondered if she should shake her loose, then decided that would be even more noticeable than leaving her where she was.

"I don't think we've met," Kate said, staring disapprovingly at Frédérique over her drooping glasses. Frédérique pouted and moved closer to Oats.

"I don't think you have, either," Oats replied with an ineffectual grin.

"Can I talk to you alone?" Kate asked, impatiently adjusting her glasses.

"Sure," Oats responded reluctantly. "Don't you go away, now," she told Frédérique with a jaunty wink.

"Oats," Kate said as they stepped down from the dance floor. "Would you please tell me what you're doing?"

"Just having a little fun," Oats shrugged.

"You've picked her up, haven't you?"

"Come on, Kate. Whatever gives you that idea?" Oats said brazenly, sneaking a look at Frédérique to make sure she wasn't making eyes at anybody else.

"Well, look who's here without her keeper," commented Kate's girlfriend Maxine. She handed Kate a glass of mineral water, keeping a bottle of beer for herself.

It wasn't funny, not under the circumstances, but Oats decided to be diplomatic and refrain from cutting down Maxine where she stood. Where did Kate dig up these puny, inadequate specimens of womanhood, she wondered, conveniently forgetting that she had introduced the two of them last fall.

"Just give me a minute, Maxine," Kate requested.

"Sure, babe. I wouldn't want to jeopardize any state secrets, would I, now?" Maxine said.

Oats watched her wander off and start talking to a couple of dykes hunched over the bar. "What's the matter with her? She's pretty chippy tonight."

"Don't worry about her. And don't try to change the subject," Kate said sternly. "Oats, are you really going to do this to Melba?"

Oats shifted her weight from one foot to the other. She wanted to tell Kate that she had no intention of doing anything to anybody, but that wasn't true, and anyway, Kate knew her too well to believe it. Kate had seen that particular gleam in her eye often enough to realize that Oats was lost, a predator with blood already staining her hands. It was too bad, because she didn't particularly want Kate to witness her fall from grace. Not that Kate would tell Melba; she was too loyal for that. But she would certainly put Oats through hell for being unfaithful, and make it much harder for Oats to ignore what she'd done.

"What can I say?" Oats replied slowly. "You know me."

"I thought you'd changed … "

"So let's leave Romeo here to her latest conquest and do a little dancing," Maxine urged, looping her arm around Kate's shoulder.

"I'll call you," Kate promised, momentarily resisting Maxine's tug toward the dance floor.

"I'll be looking forward to it," Oats replied with false bravado.

"I'm sure you will," Kate said dryly. "I'm sure you will."

Oats grimaced and waved her off. Enough was enough, after all.

"Come on, babe," Maxine said plaintively, giving Kate's hand another tug.

Kate tugged back and moved closer to Oats. "You shouldn't, you know," she said in a low voice.

Oats looked uncomfortable.

"Not that I've ever been able to convince you to change your mind when you've decided to make a fool of yourself," Kate added, her eyes hard to meet.

"You know me too well," Oats chuckled uneasily.

"The minute you get horny your brain atrophies."

"Don't go all technical on me, now," Oats said, trying to lighten things up a little.

"Seriously, Oats. Why don't you reconsider?"

Oats rolled her eyes to avoid looking at Kate. Of course she should reconsider. As a matter of fact, she'd been reconsidering all night long, but to no avail. She should have her head examined for rotting brains. Nurse or not, Kate was right; her common sense always disappeared the minute she got horny. "I think I'm going to be bad," she admitted. "You know."

"Oh, I certainly know, but I don't believe it," Kate responded heatedly. "How can you be so stupid?"

"My middle name," Oats said lightly. "Anyway, why don't you go dance with Maxine before she pulls your arm off?"

"And you? Where are you going?"

"Home," Oats whispered.

"Oh, Oats," Kate said, looking sorrowful.

"Hey, it's not the end of the world," Oats protested, even though she knew that if Melba found out, it would certainly be the end of their relationship. Well, maybe. She wasn't sure how Melba would react. All she knew was that Melba was a straightforward kind of person; she didn't beat around the bush about things. And when Oats had said she wanted to be monogamous too, Melba had believed her. In fact, Oats had believed herself. Well, it had been true at the time; what else could anybody want?

"You're so dumb," Kate said angrily.

"You're telling me?" Oats replied apologetically, but Kate was having none if it. Oats grimaced and watched her follow Maxine to the dance floor.

If life was fair, somebody else would have come along and snatched up the very attractive and very available Frédérique, but no, she was still waiting where Oats had left her. It was fate, then. Pure and simple fate that she was going to gamble her future on a whim, on a night with a woman she didn't know. And perhaps would never want to. "Ready?" Oats asked, giving Frédérique's arm a little squeeze.

"Bien sûr," Frédérique responded, smiling back at Oats. I hope this is going to be worth it, Oats mused, bending to brush her lips across Frédérique's to regain the passion Kate had scolded from her mind. "Let's get out of here," she said harshly.

Oats hailed a taxi on the street, and then ignored the driver's presence as she leaned over Frédérique and kissed her open, receptive mouth. She moaned softly, spurring Oats to an assertive exploration of her lush body. That's better, Oats thought as the taxi stopped in front of her house. If she was going to cheat on Melba, she was determined to get something memorable in return.

"Damn lock," Oats muttered, too horny to deal with her key. "Come on," she urged Frédérique when the door finally opened. She slammed the door shut and they fell toward each other, groping. Oats' leather jacket, Frédérique's winter coat, their tuques, scarfs and gloves swiftly littered the floor. Waves of passion rocked Oats' body; she felt weak-kneed with desire. "This way," she whispered urgently, leading Frédérique down the long hall to her bedroom.

"What do you like?" Oats asked, undressing Frédérique, then herself.

"Tu sais ... you know," Frédérique replied.

Oats smiled because Frédérique was right; she did know. Somehow, she always knew.

Once they were both naked, she paused to study Frédérique's body. "Nice," she whispered. "Marvellous," she added, pushing Frédérique down on the bed.

And it was nice. In fact, it was fantastic. Frédérique was eager, receptive, responsive. "Take it," Oats finally urged between clenched teeth, feeling close to the edge herself. A little later, after a satisfyingly sharp orgasm, she rose on her elbows and grinned down at Frédérique. "Was it good?" she asked, although she already knew the answer.

"Mais oui," Frédérique replied. "Was it good for you too?" she asked in accentless English.

Oats took a deep breath to slow her racing heart and rolled off Frédérique to the damp sheets beside her. "Yeah," she replied, wiping the sweat from her forehead. And along with her body, her lust began to chill. What was wrong with her? Did she always have to act out her feelings, no matter how inappropriate they were, no matter what the consequences? Why did she always feel so desperate, as if the next woman was going to be the last? Did she need to prove that she could cruise successfully every waking minute of her life?

"Do you mind if I smoke?" Frédérique asked, getting up.

Yes. Melba didn't like smoke in the bedroom. But then, Melba wouldn't like another woman in the bedroom either, especially when she was in bed with Oats. "No, I don't mind. Go ahead." She watched Frédérique remove a pack of cigarettes from her purse and light up as she walked back to the bed.

"You like me, huh?"

"You bet," Oats replied, averting her eyes as she lit her own cigarette. And it was true; she did like Frédérique. She made Oats feel like the world's best lover. If she planned to keep cheating on Melba, which of course she had no intention of doing, there would be no lack of variations on a theme to explore with this woman. Whoa, baby! Oats took a deep drag on her cigarette and coughed the thought of future faithlessness right out of her mind. What did it mean that she couldn't stay guilty for more than a couple of thoughts in a row? Sure, Frédérique was attractive, but what about the last six months and all those promises she had made to Melba?

"You've got something on your mind?" Frédérique said suggestively, leaning over and playfully blowing smoke at Oats.

You'd better believe it, although it isn't what you think. "You," Oats replied with a tired smile. After all, she couldn't tell Frédérique what she was really thinking. That whispered "you" precipitated another round of lovemaking, and by the time they were gasping for breath and bathed in sweat and trembling from the intensity of their most recent orgasms, Oats was too tired to feel guilty.

"Sleep tight, cherie," Frédérique whispered, and the last thing Oats wondered before she fell asleep was where Frédérique had learned to speak such colloquial English.

"Wake up, Sue."

"Huh?" Oats responded groggily. She turned over without opening her eyes. She must be dreaming; after all, Melba was in Toronto with her sister.

"Sue, wake up."

Melba was the only one who called her Sue, but she could still be dreaming. Right?

"Who was she?"

Wrong. This was no dream; Oats never got into this kind of trouble in her dreams. And where was Frédérique? Panic spread through her body, filled her throat, choked her awake. Oats bolted to a sitting position and opened her eyes, squinting in the harsh glare of the overhead light, promising herself for the millionth time that she'd buy a shade for that naked lightbulb the next time she was in a hardware store. She glanced beside her, but Frédérique wasn't there. Oats was alone in the bed, with Melba standing vigilance over her, her brown eyes colder than the vacuum of outer space.

"What are you doing here?" Oats asked, fretting about Frédérique. Maybe she was going to emerge from the bathroom any second now to the liquid chorus of the flushing toilet, pink and glossy in splendid nakedness, a smouldering cigarette dangling from her pouting lips.

Or perhaps Melba had already found her wandering around the apartment, had thrown her out and was now set on extracting vengeance. It didn't bear thinking about. She grabbed a blanket from the bottom of the bed and covered her body, feeling chilly and vulnerable under Melba's cool scrutiny. The wool scratched uncomfortably at her skin, and she began shivering, more from anxiety than anything else.

"My sister was in false labour. After it stopped, I decided to come home. And I *was* under the impression that I lived here," Melba replied sarcastically.

"You know what I mean," Oats said uneasily, reaching for her cigarettes.

"You're not supposed to smoke in here," Melba reminded her.

She lit up anyway; after what she'd already done in the bedroom that night, a little bit of smoke wasn't going to make much difference.

"Who was she?" Melba asked again, sitting on the edge of the bed.

Oats shrugged and avoided Melba's hurt expression, puffing hard on her cigarette. Strictly speaking, Oats didn't know exactly who Frédérique was; they had only met tonight, and neither of them had done much talking. But she couldn't say anything of the kind to Melba; it was far too flip, not to mention insulting. She had more respect for Melba than that. And anyway, when monogamy was the subject, talk was cheap. It was the sex that was expensive, and it could certainly cost her this relationship. Maybe she should tell an outright lie and deny everything. Then again, Melba probably wouldn't believe her.

"She left a note on the kitchen table," Melba said, as if she could read Oats' mind.

Oats groaned.

"A very explicit note," Melba added curtly.

She was dead. Shot right out of the water.

Melba smoothed out a crumpled piece of paper and placed it on the bed. It sat there between them like a thick, glass wall, cutting the room in two, cutting them in two. Oats could see Melba, but she couldn't touch her. She was physically incapable of reaching beyond that scrap of paper, that concrete evidence of her betrayal. Oats wanted to mutter how sorry she was, but the note silenced her. Atonement was necessary but impossible. How could she tell Melba that she would never do it again when that was all she had ever done?

"I'll pick up my things in the morning." Melba rose carefully, as if the gravity in the room had suddenly shifted, leaving her off balance.

"Don't go," Oats murmured, dropping the blanket.

"Under the circumstances, I can't very well stay."

"Please, Melba. I'm sorry," Oats said contritely, getting up, reaching out to touch her. She loved Melba too much for her to leave.

"That's not enough, Sue. I believed you. I trusted you."

"But I love you," Oats protested as Melba turned away from both her words and her touch.

"How can you say that when this room smells like a bordello, our bed stinks of sex and the sheets reek of another woman's perfume? What does love have to do with what went on here tonight?"

Oats opened her mouth to reply but nothing came out.

"Well?"

"But I do love you," Oats whispered. "Look, Melba, please stay. We'll work it out somehow."

"Oh, I'll work it out, all right. By myself," Melba added bitterly, her face tight with anger.

Oats watched her leave, feeling slightly sick to her stomach. She fell back on the rumpled sheets and lit another cigarette, as empty inside as a hollow-core door. The world's dumbest dyke, that was her. How could she have been so stupid? She butted out her cigarette and half-heartedly rearranged the rumpled sheets. Maybe Melba would think it over once she calmed down. Maybe she would give her a second chance. Not that this make her feel any better, because she had been wrong, and she knew it. She didn't like herself very much at the moment. And try as she did, nothing seemed to ease the sense of despair which slowly invaded her mind like an icy draught seeping through a leaky window on a long, cold winter's night.

# Pool Shock

**"D**amn!" Her opponent cursed plaintively as the ball rolled swiftly across the green felt, missed the pocket by a fraction of an inch and careened off the far wall.

Jock tapped the toe of her new, shiny boot in time to the music, took a deep drag on her cigarette and choked back a cough. Darn things; she appreciated the image but didn't think she'd ever get used to smoking. Cigarettes tasted horrible no matter what brand she bought — the smoke got in her eyes and made them sore, and she'd had such a lousy headache for the past week that she hadn't been able to study. Her pal Tony told her that was because smoking causes oxygen deprivation, but Jock privately (and sometimes publicly, depending on Tony's nerd quotient on any given day) thought it was impossible to take Tony seriously, even when she was probably right.

"It's all yours," her opponent said, backing away from the pool-table. Jock was intimidated; her opponent looked as tough as nails, her expressionless face tanned to tight leather despite the fact that it was the middle of the winter, her minimalist black pants and black tee-shirt outlining a thin but muscular, no-nonsense body. Still, Jock was no expert, so how could she be certain that this woman was as untouchable as she looked? Maybe under that tough exterior beat a heart of gold and a sensitive, passionate nature which was particularly vulnerable to a young, inexperienced, and unfortunately virginal dyke like Jock.

On the other hand, maybe not. "Right," Jock said. She picked up her cue and parked her cigarette on the edge of the pool table, hoping it wouldn't fall off and burn anything expensive. If there was anything expensive to burn in this ratty bar. Imagine calling a bar Ruff, something that sounded like the rather disgusting sound her dog made when she was about to throw up. But her roommate Jo had assured her it was simply another way of saying "rough," as in rough and ready. And you couldn't really call a bar "Rough," could you? Jock had wanted to know why not, since "Rough" seemed perfectly fine to her. Jo had sighed impatiently, looking at Jock like she suspected she had smoked a hole in her brains, and told her that "rough" was too literal. Whereupon Jock had opined that women had the right to know, after all, to which Jo had replied that any dyke with a modicum of common sense would clearly understand what "ruff" meant. Jock had ignored the implication because her feelings were already hurt and she hadn't wanted to tempt fate; life was too chancy as it was.

Jock rubbed chalk on the end of her cue, wrinkled her forehead as if in deep concentration, and paced slowly around the table, hoping people would think that she knew what she was doing but not betting on it. She felt so silly. The woman in black had asked her in a rather desultory fashion if she wanted to play, and Jock hadn't dared refuse, even though she wasn't quite silly enough to believe she was being invited to partake in anything more than a game of pool. But hope beats eternal, especially when you're a virgin. Oh well. She stifled a sigh, called out a number, did her best to line up the ball, and then gave it her best shot. And missed. Surprise, surprise.

"Back to you," Jock announced laconically, picking up her cigarette and taking another miserable puff. If she sank one ball tonight it would be a minor miracle. They would have to dedicate a corner of the bar as a shrine in her honour, or something. She didn't think she'd ever get the hang of this game. The pool hall in her home town had been over the barbershop, and the guys who hung out there hadn't taken kindly to girls dropping by unless it was to smuggle them a couple beers or bring them a fresh pack of cigarettes or stand around looking sleazy and screwable. Jock had never mastered the art of sleaze, and, needless to say, she hadn't particular wanted to screw the guys in the poolhall (or any others, for that matter), so she never did learn to play pool, although she doubted if the straight girls did either. And since she hadn't played more than half a dozen games since she started at McGill, why on earth had she courted humiliation by saying yes to this inscrutable dyke? What if this was how she interviewed perspective lovers? Such a stupid way to fail, without a chance to pucker up or anything! She paced unobtrusively, thinking unpleasant thoughts while her opponent bopped purposefully around the table, sinking the rest of the balls with deadly accuracy.

"Want to play another?"

Jock put out her cigarette on the floor and nodded with a careless shrug; two bucks a game wasn't going to bankrupt her. She might be a lousy player, but the one thing about pool which she did understand was that you had to act like you didn't care. The woman in black gave her a grin, racked the balls, took quick and sure aim and sank another string while Jock continued to smile, her eyes unfocused. I really don't care, she thought. It's no big deal if I lose this game or even the next. Playing pool is just a way to pass the time. It's not as if I have anything better to do. And if I lose ten bucks, well, I just won't eat lunch for a week.

Food didn't matter; being a virgin at nineteen did. And the longer they played, the more certain Jock grew that the woman in black wasn't interested in her. Why was she still a virgin when her roommate Jo was making it with everybody in sight? Well, maybe not quite. But Jo had been to bed with Betty, an older woman she met at l'Entr'acte when they had travelled to Montreal to play in the regional basketball tournament last year. And now she was tight with that punk Blue, who had seduced her one night last fall in the back yard of the bar in the pouring rain!

Jo wasn't anything special. Sure, she was cute, but in Montreal, good-looking women were a dime a dozen. Still, women were attracted to Jo like bees to honey. Jock certainly was, but that was beside the point. Why would an older woman like Betty be interested in Jo? Chemistry? A taste for young things? Jock didn't know. But she was certain that somebody fifteen years older wouldn't even bother take a second look at her. She could probably get undressed and shove her itsy-bitsy breasts right under her nose and she'd probably ask about those stupid hairs growing around her nipples or make some dumb comment about her funny-looking belly button. And if Jock had stripped off her clothes to fool around with a woman out behind the bar, she probably would have been arrested for indecent exposure. Instead, Jo had got away with it and was now dating Blue on a regular basis.

Talk about life being unfair! Jock had been certain that everything would change once she escaped from her parents and that moribund small town she and Jo had grown up in. She had thought that she would meet lots of interesting women, that living in the big city would be exciting, that she would soon have a whole string of lovers. Or one, just one. But she hadn't even come close. To add insult to injury, she hadn't made the varsity basketball team either. And after sharing a room with Jo for a term, she was even more hopelessly in love with her than she had been when they were in high school. But of course it was useless; Jo didn't have a clue how she felt.

"Are you going to play, or are you waiting for a special invitation or the second coming or what?" growled the woman in black.

She had a big mouth for such a skinny woman. Actually, Jock thought that was probably the most attractive thing about her. She snarled half-heartedly to hide her embarrassment, picked up her cue and tried to look intrepid, all the while wondering how the woman in black kept her cigarette so firmly wedged in the corner of her mouth. Maybe she practised in front of the mirror. Maybe she spit on the tip so that it would stick. Then how did she keep it from tearing half the skin off her lip when she took it out? Aw, who cared, anyway? She was probably born with a smoking butt dangling from her lips, à la James Dean. Jock grimaced at the thought and missed her shot.

"Hey, Jock, I wondered where you were," Jo said, slipping between several spectators who were too comatose to go away and do something better.

"Just getting creamed," Jock replied with false cheerfulness, wondering absently where Blue was.

"Then why are you playing?" Jo asked with impeccable logic, smiling at the woman in black, who smiled back.

"Hi, Jo."

Jock watched as the woman in black held out her hand and Jo gave it a firm shake. What was it with Jo? Did she know everybody in the whole damn city?

"Hi, Candy."

Candy? Candice? A butch like that with a name like Candy? She had to be kidding!

"So how's it going?" The woman in black — aka Candy — asked Jo with typical dyke originality, carefully laying her pool cue across the table, abandoning that particular game in favour of a potentially more interesting one. It was so transparent that Jock felt embarrassed.

"Just great," Jo responded.

"Did you teach your pal here to play pool?" Candy asked, gesturing dismissively in Jock's direction.

"Not guilty," Jo replied, grinning.

"I didn't think so. Actually, I bet you play a great game of pool," Candy added with a smile.

Hey, come on! Were they going to flirt like she wasn't even there?

She was tired of being left out, of being treated like somebody's little sister.

"Not really," Jo replied evenly.

Candy's smile went back to wherever smiles like that come from, and Jock's resentment faded.

"Want to have a beer, Jock?" Jo asked.

"But we're in the middle of a game," Candy protested.

"Oh. Sorry," Jo said, but Jock could tell that she really wasn't.

"Sure," Jock replied, relieved to escape. She gave Candy an apologetic grin and followed Jo to the bar. "She was coming on to you," she confided in Jo.

"No kidding," Jo replied dryly.

"No, I mean it!" Jock exclaimed.

"Hey, I wasn't born yesterday," Jo said. "But one woman in my life is enough, thank you very much."

Was there trouble in paradise, Jock wondered as the bartender placed two foaming beers in front of them.

"I think that Blue is seeing somebody else," Jo said.

"No!" Jock responded, shocked. She handed the bartender her last ten dollar bill and tried to think of something sympathetic to say. Nothing came to mind, and she felt inadequate, which was becoming an all too familiar feeling. Did Jo want to be comforted? Did she want her to tear a strip off Blue? Jock had never liked Blue; she thought she was selfish, all wrapped up in herself. But maybe that was the truth and maybe it wasn't; Jock was in no position to tell, because she was in love with Jo and incapable of being an impartial observer. She felt jealous of Jo's lovers even though she knew it was a total waste of time. Jo didn't even know she existed, not *that* way.

"Yes. I'm pretty sure that she's seeing another woman," Jo said.

Jock sipped her beer and tried to look sympathetic, but since that was an adult expression and she was only nineteen and still a virgin, she hadn't had much practice. "So tell me about it," she said.

"There's not much to tell," Jo replied. "But I know she's been cheating on me."

"No kidding," Jock said, impressed that Jo, who was the same ripe old age as she was, knew about stuff like that. It was all beyond her. "Is it serious?" she asked, uncharitably hoping that it was even though she knew that Jo would be hurt if Blue left her for another woman.

"I don't think so," Jo replied.

How does she know, Jock wondered? And why was she always anxiously hovering on the outside looking in while her friends dated, mated, broke up and understood imponderables with the same ease you could pluck apples off a tree in early September?

"But I don't really know for sure," Jo added.

Would this be an inappropriate time for her to tell Jo how she felt? What if she disguised her true intentions, and casually suggested a movie one night next week or dinner somewhere inexpensive on the weekend? Or what if she simply asked if she could walk Jo home tonight, back to the cosy little room they shared, where she had tucked away half a bottle of cheap red plonk left over from the time she and Tony had tried to tie one on but had ended up with headaches before they got decently spiffed?

"Hi, honey."

Speak of the devil. "It's Blue," she told Jo quite unnecessarily, turning around to look at Jo's lover, pink spikes and all. Jo shouldn't be dating a punk, Jock decided, although she had to admit that Blue was cute in spite of her deranged hair and her weird punk duds.

"Hi."

They should join the debating society and see the world, Jock thought sarcastically as Jo and Blue stared wordlessly at each other.

"Come on, babe," Blue said finally. "Let's dance."

"Yeah, go dance," Jock seconded, wanting to mope alone. She should have known better than to indulge in useless dreams. And anyway, Jo would never get involved with a childhood friend. Jo had seen her naked and sweaty in grungy locker rooms, had bandaged angry, pus-filled blisters on Jock's ugly toes, had held her as she dry heaved into a grimy school toilet because she had played the whole game and was completely exhausted. She didn't stand a chance against all these sophisticated city women with their professionally cut hair, their carefully chosen clothes and their trendy conversations.

She watched Blue lead Jo to the dance floor and then turned around and faced the bottles lining the mirrored back wall of the bar, not wanting to see them dancing together. She smoked a cigarette and drank some beer, feeling lonely. A passionate French torch song made her yearn for something she couldn't articulate. Why didn't Jo realize how she felt? Why couldn't they be more than friends? Their shared past wouldn't matter if only Jo would notice her as a woman. If only *someone* would notice her as a woman!

"Hi again. Mind if I sit here?"

Jock shrugged.

"I never did get your name," Candy said, gesturing to the bartender for a beer.

"Jock."

"You're kidding!"

"What?"

"Never mind," Candy said hastily.

Okay, I won't, Jock decided, uncharacteristically giving Candy the benefit of the doubt.

"So do you want to play some more pool?"

"I don't know," Jock replied. "I mean, I'm not very good at it."

"You're telling me," Candy said with a friendly grin.

"I guess you just want to take the rest of my hard-earned money," Jock joked, watching Candy light a cigarette.

"You bet."

Jock finished her beer while Candy sat patiently beside her, blowing perfect smoke rings and nodding in time to the music. Is she coming on to me, Jock wondered? Naw, she just wants a sucker to beat at pool. Or maybe she wants to dance. Or go to bed with me. "I gotta go," Jock said abruptly, getting up from her stool.

"Oh?"

"Yeah."

"How about giving me your phone number, then?"

Jock froze in amazement as Candy pulled a tattered scrap of paper from her pocket and asked the bartender for a pen. "I live in a dorm," she sputtered.

"So?"

Jock looked at her for a moment, then leaned over the counter, wrote her name and number in block letters, and gave Candy back the paper. Candy squinted at it for a couple of seconds, nodded in satisfaction and shoved the paper into her pants pocket. "I'll give you a call sometime."

"Sure," Jock replied, trying to sound casual.

"Maybe we can play another game of pool."

Was she kidding? She stared at Candy, but it was too dark to tell. "Any time," she said, as unsure of her meaning as she sounded.

Candy smiled knowingly, slid off the stool and nodded goodbye, turning back toward the pool table. Jock watched her challenge another dyke to a game and then headed for the door, musing about cowardice while she waited for the coat check girl to find her coat.

"Merci." She tossed a couple of quarters into the wicker basket the coat-check woman used for tips.

"De rien."

Jock buttoned her coat, wrapped her scarf around her neck, pulled her tuque over her short, brown hair and left the bar. It was cold and still snowing. She slipped into her gloves and clapped her hands together. The newly fallen snow sparkled, lighting up the night. She clapped her hands again, feeling as dull as the resulting snow-muffled echo. Why did Candy want her phone number? After all, Candy liked Jo. Everybody liked Jo, but Jo wasn't available.

What was wrong with her? She was nearly twenty years old, and she didn't have a lover. She should have taken Candy's phone number too; that way she wouldn't have to wait for her to call. Still, anything could happen between now and then; Jo could tire of Blue and fall madly in love with Jock or Jock could fall madly in love with someone else, someone she didn't even know yet … But there was no future in fantasizing about impossibilities. And anyway, Candy would probably lose that little piece of paper with her number on it, and even if she didn't, Jock's handwriting would fade after a couple of washings. And even if Candy never washed her jeans, the paper itself would eventually turn into lint. Or Candy would find Jock's number a couple weeks from now and not even remember who she was. Or worse yet, remember and not care.

She could confront her fears, turn around, and go back to the bar. What was the worse thing that could happen? Candy might laugh at her. Or Candy might want to take her home to bed. Which possibility was she more afraid of?

Jock stuck out her tongue and captured a snowflake. What a dumb bunny I am, she thought, trudging alone through a mid-winter snowstorm when I could be dancing with Candy, touching Candy, maybe even making love with Candy. She buried her gloved hands deep in her coat pockets and bent her head to cut the wind. Such a dumb bunny to have fled like Cinderella at the stroke of midnight, especially when she knew that there would be no princess running after her to beg her to change her mind.

# Charades

**B**lue almost choked on her beer when Jo asked, "How many times do you figure you've made love in your life?"

"How the hell should I know? I mean, I don't keep track," Blue sputtered, wiping her mouth with the back of her hand.

"Oh come on; you're not that much older than me, and I know exactly how many times I've made love," Jo replied, putting her bottle down on the counter.

"I've never thought about it," Blue replied impatiently.

No, Blue wouldn't bother to keep count, Jo decided somewhat uncharitably. Especially if she was living a double life, sleeping with two women at the same time. "A woman of the world, right?" Jo said recklessly. Damn the torpedoes, and all that. She *had* to know. Maybe.

"Yeah, right," Blue replied, her face averted.

So go away and leave me alone, Jo thought bitterly. We'll simply spend the evening pretending that nothing's wrong. She watched two older women on l'Entr'acte's dance floor, absently following their synchronized, fleet-footed moves.

"Let's dance," Blue said abruptly.

Does she think that dancing will make it better, Jo wondered? Or that I'll stop cross-examining her if I get horny? How well she knows me, she thought dejectedly.

They claimed a tiny space next to the floor-to-ceiling mirror and danced close to a torch song by Martine St-Clair. It was one of Jo's favourites, which didn't improve her state of mind.

"That's better. You're so prickly tonight," Blue whispered, nuzzling her neck.

And it's not my period, Jo refrained from retorting. As if Blue cared.

Their bodies moved together to the music; Blue's breasts grazed hers, and Blue's firm thighs circled enticingly. Jo's anger gradually seeped away, and she gave in and wrapped her arms around Blue, running her fingers up and down her spine. Alienation stinks, she thought. "Want to come home with me?" she asked.

"To the dorm?" Blue replied absently. "What about your roommate?"

"Jock? Oh, don't worry about her. She can bunk down with Tony again."

"Nasty girl, kicking your roommate out like that. Have you no loyalty?" Blue teased.

Jo shivered with arousal when Blue's hands slid between their bodies and ran lightly over her breasts. "Jock won't care. And I want you," she whispered fiercely, rubbing her body against Blue. I love you, she thought. I love you, dammit. Something shifted in Blue's eyes and Jo silently rejoiced; she had finally stopped thinking about her other lover.

"Sounds good to me," Blue said. "Let's go."

Jo followed Blue from the dance floor through the crowd of women clustered around the bar and out the front door, her winter jacket unzipped, her scarf trailing behind her. Breathless from the sudden shock of the cold, they gulped icy air as they ran for the bus which had stopped for a red light at the corner.

"How are your courses going?" Jo asked. They sat in the back, not touching. Jo studiously avoided looking at the straight couple passionately necking in the seat in front of them, but it was impossible to completely ignore them. It made her furious that men and women could touch, kiss and otherwise grope in public, while if she and Blue indulged, they would probably be arrested. Or get beat up. If it was okay for straight couples, why wasn't it okay for them?

"You want to talk about school at this time of night?" Blue asked, her eyebrows raised.

"Not if you don't want to," Jo replied swiftly, afraid that resorting to small talk given her away. She watched as realization dawned in Blue's eyes. And guilt, miserable, tell-tale guilt. It must be true, then. Blue was involved with another woman.

Jo turned and looked out the window, seeing nothing but her own pale shadow reflected in the dirty glass as the bus slowly traversed the icy, dimly lit streets. Blue was steadily withdrawing, and Jo was growing increasingly afraid that she was in love with someone else. What other explanation could there be for her absentmindedness, her moodiness, her impatience with things which had previously charmed her? Blue's interest was waning, evaporating like dew in the hot sun, and no matter what she did, Jo couldn't stop this steady attrition.

What made Jo feel even worse was that in her desperation to salvage her relationship with Blue, she was treating Jock badly. It didn't matter that Jock never complained, that she took the abuse without comment. Jock had been her best friend since they were toddlers, and she didn't deserve it. Just because Blue was hurting her didn't mean that she had to hurt Jock, especially not now. Jock was going through a difficult time: flunking most of her courses, failing to make the basketball team, simultaneously dealing with loneliness, sexual frustration and one hell of a crush on her. Not that Jock was really in love with her, Jo rationalized. Once she got a taste of the real thing, she would put those schoolgirl dreams behind her. But still, she ought to be nicer to her.

She sighed and reached up and tugged on the sagging cord, then stood and walked to the door, grabbling a rail as the bus bumped to a halt. Damn potholes. You could lose a small car down one, even in winter. The door snapped open and she and Blue jumped to the snow-covered curb. The brittle snow crunched dryly underfoot. It sounds just like my soul breaking in two, Jo thought.

"God, it's cold," Blue said.

"I despise winter," Jo announced nervously.

"Me too."

"Anyway, here we are," Jo said cheerfully. Small talk about the weather, yet! This was going to be awful. Maybe they should forget about the whole thing. But she didn't say anything as they climbed the snow-covered steps, opened the heavy door and walked into the overheated foyer. Jo unwound her scarf, opened her coat and stamped her booted feet on the mat. Clots of grimy snow loosened, dropped off and immediately started to melt. She opened the inner door, her nose twitching involuntarily at the smell of industrial-strength disinfectant, the stale aroma of cooked cabbage and a certain eau de damp woollen sock which pervaded the women's residence.

"Talking about school, I only have one course this term," Blue said.

Jo waved at the monitor on duty at the switchboard. "Are you ever lucky! I've even got one Saturday mornings!" Jo moaned, letting herself slip into that neutral and therefore safe topic.

"That's first year for you," Blue said. "But don't forget, I have my thesis to write."

"Are you going to finish it this year?" Jo asked as they waited for the elevator, standing beside a woman in a faded blue housecoat, her hair in plastic curlers.

"I doubt it," Blue replied. The three of them entered the elevator, where the smell of cabbage grew stronger. The woman in the blue housecoat ignored them, staring at the smudged, scratched door. Maybe she didn't like dykes. Or pink-haired punks like Blue. Or both. Jo turned and winked at Blue, but Blue was off somewhere ethereal, her eyes blank.

Damn her! Jo placed her hand on Blue's behind, squeezing hard. Blue jumped with surprise and gave Jo a quizzical look, then grinned and leaned back into her hand. "You've got some nerve," she said with a husky laugh after blue housecoat got off on the second floor and the doors closed again.

"You ain't seen nothing yet," Jo promised, releasing Blue's bottom after one final squeeze.

Jo was relieved that Jock wasn't in their room. She was probably down the hall at Tony's, the two of them commiserating over their singular lack of success with women. Jo was very horny. Blue had always excited her, but since she had realized that she had competition, she couldn't seem to get enough. Jo kissed her passionately, her tongue searching urgently, her body straining against Blue's like she wanted to get inside.

"Why don't we finish this in bed?" Blue said gruffly.

"Wait," Jo said. She watched Blue sit on the edge of the bed, then draped her shirt over the back of a chair and dropped her jeans on top.

"For what?"

"Just stay like that," Jo added, falling down on her knees in front of Blue.

"Oh, god," Blue groaned.

"Do you like this?" Jo asked between licks, knowing very well how much Blue liked it.

"What do you think?" Blue muttered, impatiently grasping Jo's head and pulling her all the way in. She fell back on the bed with a long, drawn-out groan.

"I love you," Jo whispered as Blue came. She was such a coward that the only place she felt safe admitting her love for this woman was between her thighs, when she was coming so hard that she couldn't possibly hear anything but the harsh sound of her own breathing.

"I want you too," Blue whispered, pulling Jo down on the bed.

"Blue."

"What?"

"Do you love me?"

Blue's abruptly stopped and sat up. The sexual tension between them evaporated like gasoline spattered on hot pavement, and Jo grew still. I shouldn't have asked, she thought. I should have taken what she was willing to give, no more, no less. I shouldn't have believed that the power of sex was enough to force her hand. She has never said that she loved me, not once in the past five months. And fool that I was, I told her I loved her the minute I knew, right after we made love in the rain out behind l'Entr'acte that chilly September night we met. "Sorry," she said miserably.

"You don't have to be sorry," Blue responded immediately.

Jo shrugged, got up and put on her shirt. It was January, the coldest damn month of the year, and she was freezing. "You're seeing someone else," she stated flatly, turning to face Blue, who was still sitting naked on the bed, seemingly oblivious to the cold air blowing through the dry, cracked calking around the aluminum windows.

"Yes," Blue replied after a long silence.

"Do you want to break up?"

"No," came the response after an equally long pause.

Jo turned away, picked up a tattered, half-empty pack of cigarettes from the cluttered desk and shook one out. She stuck it in the corner of her mouth, found a pack of matches and lit it, drawing the acrid smoke into her mouth. "Yuk," she muttered, coughing as smoke filled her throat and lungs. How could people smoke? She tried again with the same result, and put the cigarette out. "What do you want, then?" She used the flattened butt of the cigarette to draw pictures in the grey ash; lines, circles, squares. The ashtray smelled stale, like l'Entr'acte at the beginning of the evening, before too many cigarettes were smoked, before too much beer was spilled on the perpetually stained floor.

"I don't know," Blue replied.

"Well, that's helpful then, isn't it?" Jo retorted, resolutely taking another cigarette from Jock's pack and lighting it, as if to punish herself for being unable to change something which was not her fault. This time she didn't inhale so much smoke, but it still tasted bad. "How long has this been going on?"

"Look, Jo, I never meant to hurt you." Blue rose from the bed and collected her clothes from the floor.

"Sure."

"No, I mean it."

Jo smoked in silence, watching Blue dress. Well, now she knew for sure. But there was no satisfaction in knowing, and nothing to do with the knowledge, nothing at all.

"I guess I owe you an explanation," Blue said finally.

"I guess you bloody well do."

She watched Blue sit on the edge of the bed and pull her boots on. "I met her a couple weeks after you and I started dating."

Jo turned away and repeatedly stabbed the cigarette into the ashtray. So soon, she thought? Did she ever take me seriously? "Who is she?"

"You don't know her. She's older."

"I see."

"No you don't. I mean, it doesn't have anything to do with you, with us," Blue said.

"Like hell," Jo said bitterly, lighting another cigarette and puffing angrily on it.

"I mean it. It isn't serious."

"Well, what is it, then?"

"Will you stop smoking, for god's sake? I feel guilty enough as it is!"

Jo gave her a dirty look and puffed furiously, hearing Blue sigh. "It's just sex, that's all," Blue said softly.

Had Blue really believed that particular revelation would make her feel any better? Jealously burst around her like the flames of hell, grabbing her throat with a molten fist. It was shattering to realize that Blue thought sex on the sly with another woman was more important than their relationship. Didn't she satisfy Blue sexually? Wasn't she attractive enough?

"It's different with her," Blue added, as if reading Jo's mind.

"Different?" Jo replied in a strangled voice, afraid that if she asked how, Blue would tell her.

"Suzanne is a little bit crazy. She likes to use a dildo," Blue blurted, getting up and helping herself to one of Jock's cigarettes. Jo felt like she was going to vomit. She hadn't wanted a name. She hadn't wanted details. And she hadn't wanted to hear about how they did it, afraid that such knowledge would perpetually curdle her thoughts. She had wanted to distance herself from Blue's other lover — it was the only way she could possibly cope. But now. Oh, but now. A dildo! It was too much to handle. And she had been stupid enough to think that she had been giving Blue everything she needed!

"It's just different," Blue repeated, misery written all over her face.

"I think you had better leave," Jo said, keeping her voice soft so the scream in her mind wouldn't escape. An older woman called Suzanne. With whom Blue was doing it with a dildo. Whose world was this? Certainly not the one she had planned to create for herself.

"Jo — "

"Please go."

"Jo, I'm sorry."

"So what?"

"I really am ... "

"I don't care!"

"Look, can't we talk — "

"Blue, please go. You've said too much already."

"I'll call you tomorrow."

Then the telephone will ring itself to death, Jo thought. She listened to Blue's leaving, the pungent crackling of leather as Blue slipped into her jacket, the quieter sounds as she swiftly donned scarf and gloves, the meek goodbye. And then the door clicked shut with muffled but soul-shattering finality.

Jo sat down at Jock's desk and calmly smoked the remaining cigarettes, making herself so sick that she thought she really might throw up. But after she hung her head between her thighs, the feeling passed. She opened the window to clear the smoke, wondering why Jock hadn't come home yet. She changed into her housecoat and went to the washroom, taking her facecloth and towel with her. She used the toilet, then selected the cleanest sink and washed herself thoroughly, taking comfort in the familiar smell of her soap, in the ritual of rubbing the facecloth back and forth between her thighs, soaping, then rinsing. "Gonna wash that gal right out of my hair," she muttered, then laughed rather hysterically as she towelled herself dry.

Maybe Jock would be back by now. Maybe she would go to Tony's room, smoke some more cigarettes and toss back a few beers with the two of them. Maybe she wouldn't miss Blue if she never stopped moving, if she never closed her eyes, if she never relinquished her anger. Maybe she would seduce Jock. Give her a real thrill. After all, that was what Jock wanted, wasn't it? Maybe she would seduce the both of them, orchestrate an orgy between friends. Blue had probably done it, so why shouldn't she?

She rebuttoned her housecoat, looked in the mirror, and then laughed again, this time not so hysterically. How could someone in such a tatty housecoat be capable of seducing anybody?

"Hi, Jo," Tony said, breezing into the washroom, reeking of beer and cigarettes.

"Hi. Have you seen Jock?" Jo asked, gathering up her facecloth, towel and soap dish.

"Yeah. She just staggered back to your room," Tony responded with a giggle.

"Great." Jo gave her a wave and left the washroom. Jock was probably drunk, but it was better than facing the night alone. And tomorrow night and the night after that.

Damn her.

# Heartache

**M**elba was bound to forgive her and come home soon. That forlorn hope was enough to keep Oats going. She went to work early and came home late, grateful for the change of scenery and for other people to talk to, eager to escape the oppression of her silent apartment. It spooked her. It was so quiet that she could hear the kitchen clock ticking. She discovered that the hot water faucet in the bathroom dripped. She could follow the conversations of her upstairs neighbours. And although she had lived there for years, she started waking up at night when the heating system cut in and the pipes began to knock. She hadn't realized that Melba had taken up so much space or that she had been so noisy about it. And she hadn't expected to feel this lonely. Previous love affairs had ended with predictable regularity and she had picked up the pieces and gone on with her life without much grief, but this time, it wasn't the same. But why should she be surprised? Nothing about her relationship with Melba had been familiar, so why should this particular interlude be any different? And she was sure that it was only an interlude; Melba did love her, and nobody who loved Sue Dobbs had been able to stay away for long.

One evening she unearthed the vacuum cleaner from the back of the hall closet and cleaned every speck of long-ignored dust from the furniture and copious lint balls from the hardwood floors. The next night she scoured the apartment until it was spotless. The night after that, she stuffed several overflowing piles of laundry into the washing machine and then sat up half the night waiting for them to dry. She wanted to be sure that everything was prepared when Melba's key turned in the lock.

When Frédérique called, she acted disinterested. This was no affectation — she honestly didn't care. She spurned her advances, at first gently, then somewhat brusquely when Frédérique persisted. And she didn't call Kate; she would be sympathetic, but only after she said I told you so in half a million ways, each of them more damning than the last. Oats felt guilty enough as it was. I told myself so too, she argued mentally with Kate as the long, solitary hours passed, but I didn't listen. I couldn't. All I could hear was my lust speaking and it was drowning out everything else. At that particular moment, Frédérique was the only game in town. You know how it is. How it can be. Yeah, and look where it got me.

Every night when she went to bed she convinced herself that Melba would be lying there beside her the next morning. It was the only way she could get to sleep. But the days succeeded each other in monotonous progression, and when her alarm clock woke her each dark, chilly mid-winter morning, she was still alone. Part of her life was missing, and she didn't know where it had gone. She felt as if she had fallen asleep on an airplane only to wake up in a different universe.

A week passed, then two. Oats rolled out of bed each morning, ate something for breakfast and went to work at the print shop. But her mind wasn't on her job. She made so many mistakes that her boss threatened to demote her, to put her back on simple black-and-white runs unless she smartened up. That weekend she slept in, ate too much junk food, chain-smoked, and downed too many rum and cokes. By Sunday night she wasn't so sure Melba was coming back, and Monday morning she wasn't surprised when she woke up alone.

It had snowed overnight, five or six inches of heavy snow which clotted as the temperature rose after dawn to hover near freezing. Good weather for kids to play outside, for a spirited snowball fight or for building a lopsided snowman in the back yard. Not that there were any kids downtown where Oats lived, or any backyards, for that matter.

Oats took a last puff of her cigarette and dressed slowly, laboriously, concentrating on the straightness of the seams on her old-fashioned leggings, tightening and then loosening her boot laces until they were just right, adjusting her ear muffs so good old jack frost couldn't nibble at her ear lobes. Nibbling at ear lobes made her think of Melba, an incorrigible nibbler if there ever was one. But thinking about Melba made her feel worse, so she tried to stop, albeit without much success. Her ear muffs were all tangled up and wouldn't fit right, so she impatiently tossed them back into the closet and pulled her Montreal Canadiens' tuque down over her head. She stuffed her fingers into her gloves, grabbed the shovel, and went out and got to work.

Before long Oats was sweating with exertion, her breath coming in short puffs. She didn't mind clearing the balcony and staircase when the snow was light and fluffy and there wasn't so much of it, but when it was so dense that each shovelful weighed a ton, she began to wish she had hired one of the local teenagers to do her shovelling for her.

She tossed a thick chunk of snow over the balcony and rested for a couple of minutes, leaning on the shovel. She wanted a cigarette but felt too breathless to go in and get it; to add insult to injury, she seemed to be developing a sudden and surprisingly painful case of indigestion somewhere beneath her breastbone. That would teach her not to eat a bacon-and-eggs breakfast before physical exertion. Funny, though, it didn't really feel like indigestion.

She shrugged her stiffening shoulders and raised the shovel, grimacing as the pain in her chest intensified. It was probably just her gall bladder reacting to too much grease. Kate, who was a nurse, enjoyed reminding all and sundry that Oats was a prime candidate for gall bladder problems: female, fat and forty-something. And Oats, who on principle refused to believe that she was vulnerable to anything, certainly couldn't deny that she was female, although she was closer to fifty than forty. But she wasn't all that fat; a little overweight, maybe, but who wasn't? Still, perhaps Kate was right. Maybe her gall bladder was hitting on her. Now wouldn't Kate get a kick out of that!

Oats grunted and forgot about Kate and her gall bladder and the snow as a sharp spasm blossomed and spread up her chest into her neck and shoulder. The shovel fell from her grasp but she hardly noticed, even when it slipped off the balcony and slid lazily down the snow-covered steps.

What the hell was happening? She ran her hand back and forth over her chest and tried to take a deep breath, but it wouldn't come. The harder she tried the more it hurt, and she fell on her knees, breathless, the snow turning red then black as her vision faded. She had never felt such incredible pain her life. She ripped open her coat and tore at her chest. Oh god, she thought, I'm dying. And Melba is still mad at me! And then something deep inside pumped up the volume and pain exploded like a cluster bomb, obliterating consciousness.

"And how do we feel today, Ms. Dobbs?"

Oats tried to groan, but nothing came out.

"She's coming around," somebody else said, her worried voice vaguely familiar.

Oats groaned again, and this time a rusty grunt escaped from between her dry lips. Was she still alive? She must be: she hurt too much to be dead. She opened her eyes slowly, carefully, and looked around at the dingy, paint-starved walls, at the bank of machines on the wall, some flashing, some blipping, some ominously silent, at the dozens of wires and tubes attached to or even sticking into her body. She shut her eyes tight and this time her groan sounded like one.

"And are we feeling a bit better today, Ms. Dobbs?"

We feel as if a snowplough ran over our chest and then backed up to make sure the job was properly done, Oats thought sourly, but she didn't impart this particular specimen of sick-bed humour to Miss Starched Shirt. "Water," she croaked instead.

"Thank god you're all right, Oats."

Oats opened her eyes again and slowly turned her head, seeing Kate standing by the other side of the bed, all decked out in her nursing gear, her stethoscope dangling loosely from her pocket like a restless snake. "What are you doing here?" she said unreasonably, so inexplicably unnerved at Kate's appearance that her eyes filled with tears.

"I work here, stupid," Kate replied gently, giving Oats a smile as she bent the straw in the plastic glass.

Oh. Right. She was in a hospital, Kate was a nurse, so it followed. Sort of. Oats sipped cautiously, wincing as the cool water stung her chapped lips and her raw throat. "What's wrong with me?"

"Your doctor will be here soon," Starched Shirt replied evasively.

"Why can't you tell me?" Oats asked, looking from Starched Shirt to Kate. The two nurses glanced swiftly at each other, their eyes suddenly wary. "I had a heart attack, didn't I?" Oats said, and suddenly she knew that that was exactly what had happened. But wait a minute — she was too young, only forty-seven. Maybe she was just dreaming. Sure, that was it; she was going to wake up any minute now and have a good laugh over such a stupid nightmare.

"Kate? ... "

No, she wasn't dreaming; this was all too real. But maybe it hadn't been a heart attack. Maybe it was something else, something safer, a malady you could excise nice and clean, an illness you could medicate out of existence. Something fuzzy, a conversation piece, a nuisance but not fatal. Not like a heart attack.

"Your doctor — "

"I had a heart attack, didn't I, Kate?" Oats interrupted, trusting her friend to answer truthfully.

"Yes," Kate affirmed, ignoring Starched Shirt's frown.

"Her doctor — "

"I couldn't lie once she guessed, could I?" Kate responded tiredly. Starched Shirt looked uncertain, then glanced at her watch and left the room without uttering another word.

"Oh, Kate," Oats moaned weakly, tears overflowing her eyes and running freely down her cheeks.

"It's going to be okay, Oats," Kate commiserated, but her sympathy made Oats cry even harder. Kate lowered the bar, bent over and reached for Oats, slipping her arms under the IV tubes.

"Was it bad?" Oats dared to ask.

"Bad enough," Kate admitted cautiously, squeezing her shoulder in an attempt to take the sting out of her words.

"Am I going to die?" Oats wailed.

"Of course not!" Kate exclaimed with a little laugh. "Of course not!"

Oats believed her because Kate was her friend. And disbelieved her because she was a nurse doing her job. And ended up in limbo, where the only thing left for her to do was to cry some more because she felt so sorry for herself. Kate petted her, crooning in her ear until her tears dried up. Oats sniffed one last time and decided that even if you're nearly dead, you can't spend the rest of your life snivelling about it.

"Will you call some people for me? My mother, my brother, some of my friends?"

"I already have — you've been out for over twenty-four hours," Kate said, untangling herself from Oats' IV lines.

"Twenty-four hours?"

"Yes. And I contacted the print shop and explained what happened. I called Melba, too."

"Oh yeah?" Oats tried to sit up but fell back with a gasp. All her strength was gone; her muscles felt as insubstantial as feathers.

"Yes. She said she would call me back to see how you were doing," Kate replied. "Did you two end up having a fight?"

"I cheated. She left." Oats closed her eyes to stop from crying again, but it didn't work; the tears seeped through anyway.

"I was afraid of that."

"Never mind. Just never mind," Oats responded with more energy than she felt, impatiently wiping away the tears.

"Well, I'm sure she'll come to see you," Kate said.

"I said never mind," she repeated through gritted teeth. Kate's cheerfulness was getting on her nerves. And she would get over Melba; she always got over women sooner or later.

"I've got to go now."

"Do you have to?" Oats said, panic rising at the thought of being left alone with only her defective heart for company. What if something went wrong? What if she had another heart attack? What if she died when nobody else was here? What if she was *alone* when it happened?

"Don't worry. Somebody will look in on you regularly," Kate reassured her.

"But I don't want to be alone!"

"Oats, you're not alone. You're in intensive care. You're being monitored constantly. That's what all those machines are," Kate explained patiently.

Intensive care? Oats took a closer look at the machines surrounding her bed and suddenly realized that the inner workings of her body were exposed to anybody smart enough to decipher all those blips and dots and squiggles. She felt strangely self-conscious and not at all assured.

"Don't look so alarmed. It's standard procedure to put heart attack patients in intensive care until they're stabilized."

Stabilized? Did she mean that Oats' heart was going to go ka-boom again, or what?

"Try to rest," Kate added. "That's what you need now."

But Oats knew better. What she needed now was Melba. Immediately. Or to wake up from a bad dream. Actually, in a more mundane way, what she really needed was to pee. And urgently. She haltingly mentioned this to Kate, whose professionalism rose to the occasion. She peeled back the covers, raised Oats' hospital gown and inserted the bedpan. Oats' terror of dying abated as she struggled to overcome her shyness. A couple of tense minutes later, she was successful.

"There," Kate said, whisking away the bedpan and tucking Oats in. "Now try to sleep."

"Yes, nurse," Oats replied meekly.

Kate bent down and kissed her cheek, brushed her hand across Oats' forehead and told her that she loved her. Then she gave her an injection and left the room. Oats was suddenly exhausted, too tired to care about being alone. Maybe it was the drugs, maybe it was her aching heart, maybe it was the shock of discovering that she wasn't invulnerable. Maybe it was all of those things or none of them. It didn't matter and even if it had, there wasn't anything she could do about it anyway. She felt light-headed, probably from the medication. Her sense of immortality had died an unexpected, sudden death. But she would feel better tomorrow. And by tomorrow Melba would have forgiven her, and then she wouldn't be alone any longer. She had no reason to be afraid, because she wasn't going to die. And that was a promise.

# A Night To Remember

Kate sat on the edge of the bed, squinted at herself in the oak-framed mirror hanging from the wall above her dresser, and parted her wet, shoulder-length brown hair, combing it back off her face. She cleaned her glasses and put them on, frowning at her reflection in the mirror. She looked tired, but that was no surprise; she was exhausted from working double shifts twice this past week. Nursing as a career sucked: severe, continuous cuts in government funding, overworked, demoralized staff, wards crowded with chronically ill patients and old people no longer capable of caring for themselves at home, confused, weak patients forced into the halls, their narrow beds jostled by curious, staring visitors and perpetually harried staff — why was she still working in a hospital? So many of her friends had quit in disgust, burnt out by the long hours, the horrendous responsibilities, the ever-present bureaucracy, the penny-pinching which had transformed hospitals from healthcare facilities to drab dens of hopelessness where families regularly discarded their elders and where people without money, alternatives and hope went to die. She had made an idealistic career choice, and now she was paying for it. Nursing was a thankless task; unfortunately, it was the only thing she knew how to do. How could she quit, go back to school and then establish herself in a new career on the couple of thousand dollars she had managed to save over the years? It was impossible. Besides, the local economy was so bad that if she gave up nursing, she would probably end up homeless herself, living in a shelter and depending on one of the food banks which had sprung up during the recession and which now seemed to be a permanent part of the scenery. And anyway, she didn't have enough energy to change her life. She felt too tired to even try.

So many nurses went south, lured by the promise of clean, modern hospitals outfitted with the latest in technological advances, wooed by fat contracts, comprehensive benefits packages, lengthy vacations and warm winters. Kate hadn't. The health care system in Montreal was sick (as was the rest of Canada's, for that matter), but there was something inherently wrong in making a profit on disease the way they did in the United States. There had to be another way, and despite being exhausted, demoralized and uncertain of how she could last another twenty years until she reached retirement age, she still wanted to be part of the solution rather than trying to run away from the problem.

She felt down — both physically tired and emotionally drained. She certainly wasn't looking forward to going out with Maxine tonight, not when Oats was still in the intensive care unit, hooked up to half a dozen machines which still wouldn't keep her alive if her time had come. Her heart attack had been fairly serious, and there had been permanent damage. Oats would have to change her lifestyle: stop smoking, cut down on her drinking, eat better, exercise regularly, rest more. Kate didn't know if Oats was capable of doing that. They had been close friends for over twenty-five years, since shortly after a much younger, naive and decidedly timid Kate had stepped off the train from Halifax. After months of mind-numbing isolation, Kate had found her way to a seedy bar down by the waterfront where a young, brash and sex-crazed (or so it seemed to Kate) Oats had befriended her and proceeded to initiate her into those sometimes nonsensical, often rigid and downright stupid codes of lesbian behaviour which had existed before the impact of feminism and the gay liberation movement.

You don't meet many people you stay friends with for twenty-five years, Kate mused as she got up from the bed and put on her bra and panties. They had certainly had differences of opinion, they had sometimes chased the same women, usually with disastrous results for Kate, and they had even tried to sleep together one rather drunken and dateless New Year's Eve. That particular fiasco had deepened their friendship rather than destroying it, thank God. But Oats didn't possess a sense of moderation. She cruised women as an end in itself and lived her whole life teetering on the edge. She had been wild when they met, and she was still wild in middle age. And that was the problem, Kate thought grimly; if Oats didn't tame some of that wildness, it was going to contribute to her premature death, and sooner rather than later. Maybe her naughty, no-holds-barred lifestyle kept her young in spirit, but she had never taken care of her body, with the result that her heart was already old for its age and threatening to retire from this world, taking a kicking and screaming and terrified Oats with it.

"Am I going to die?" Oats had pleaded, desperately wanting reassurance. And Kate had readily given it to her, replying "of course not." She had even been capable of faking a hearty chuckle, as if the very idea of Oats dying was absurd. A good bedside manner in the face of adversity is probably the most essential nursing skill of all, she thought cynically, pulling a tissue from the box and blowing her nose. But I'm not God, so how on earth do I know whether she's going to die? We're all going to die sometime, but that's no consolation when it's your own mortality you're staring in the face.

The telephone rang, cutting off Kate's dismal train of thought. She reached over and plucked the cordless phone from her bedside table.

"Hi sweety."

"Hi Max," she said in a subdued voice.

"Pick you up in ten minutes?"

"Max, maybe we should put it off. I'm kind of down about Oats."

"But Kate, I haven't seen you for a whole week," Maxine replied plaintively.

"I know, hon, but I'm afraid I'm not going to be very good company tonight," Kate explained.

"Please, Kate. You know how much I was looking forward to this."

"Okay," Kate sighed, giving in.

"Great! I'll be there soon, then."

Kate switched off the phone and put it back down on the dresser. It was probably better to keep busy rather than sitting at home moping about things she couldn't change. Still, she wasn't certain she had the energy to deal with Maxine tonight. Sometimes Maxine pushed too hard, wanted too much, came on too forcefully. Kate supposed she had good reason to act that way: after dating for nearly six months, they still hadn't made love, although not due to lack of trying on Maxine's part. She knew that Maxine really wanted her; she was the one who was reluctant. Every time she and Maxine hadn't seen each other for awhile, she started thinking that maybe it was time, that maybe she was being silly to resist. After all, she was no blushing virgin; she'd been around the proverbial block more than a few times. Just because her last lover had run off with a man didn't mean that Maxine was going to do the same thing. But Kate felt uneasy about giving in, and she was troubled by Maxine's unreasonable anger whenever she put a stop to their lovemaking. And by Maxine's thoughtless criticism in front of their friends and her rages whenever they had a little spat or an inconsequential difference of opinion.

Kate didn't know how to deal with Maxine's fierce temper. She did know, though, that she didn't want to be rushed. She didn't want to feel guilty about taking her own sweet time. And although she wanted the next step to be spontaneous, it never seemed to happen that way. Maxine always wanted too much too fast and too passionately.

Snap out of it, she told herself. There's no time to think about that now. Still, she had given in yet again, which didn't please her. But there it was, and Maxine was probably on her way over to pick her up right this very minute. She opened the closet door and chose a pair of black slacks and a white sweater, zipping up her slacks just as the phone rang again.

"Kate, it's Melba."

"Hold on half a sec, Melba, my doorbell's ringing," Kate replied, setting the phone back down on the dresser and rushing down the hall.

"Hi, Max — I'll just be a minute — I'm on the phone with Melba," she explained as she opened the door.

Sure," Maxine said, following Kate into her bedroom. "Mmmm. You sure smell good," she added, moving closer to Kate as she picked up the telephone.

"Max!" Kate exclaimed with an uncomfortable laugh, slipping away. "Melba? Sorry — Maxine just arrived."

"I won't keep you, Kate. I just wanted an update on Oats."

"She's better, but still in intensive care." Maxine had moved closer and was running her fingers through Kate's hair. Kate could smell liquor on Maxine's breath, and wondered absently why she had been drinking so early in the evening.

"She's still in intensive care? But it's been five days," Melba replied.

"She had a pretty serious heart attack, Melba," Kate said, gently disentangling herself from Maxine's hands, which had moved from her hair and were now sliding up and down her back.

"Come on, Kate. Let's get going," Maxine urged.

Kate covered the mouthpiece of the phone with the palm of her hand. "In a minute, Max. I can't just hang up on her."

Maxine grimaced and flopped on the bed. Kate walked over to the window. It was snowing in a desultory, windless fashion, with fluffy flakes fluttering slowly to the pavement. "She'd really like to see you, you know."

The silence was so pervasive that for a moment she thought that Melba had hung up. "Melba?"

"I'm still here. And I know that she wants to see me. But I can't forgive her for what she did."

"She's scared, she's sick, and she's alone. And she still loves you," Kate said bluntly, trying to ignore Maxine's derisive snort.

"What do you expect me to do? Stand by my woman after what she did?" Melba retorted bitterly.

Well, excuse me for living, Kate thought. "She was your lover. You lived together for nearly half a year. Surely that means something to you."

"More than you'll ever know," Melba said, her voice suddenly subdued again. "And quite obviously more than it did to Oats."

Oats could be such a damn fool. But still … "Melba, I can get you into intensive care anytime you want."

"I don't know … "

"Well, think about it and we'll talk again tomorrow," Kate said.

"Okay."

"Call me," Kate said encouragingly, but Melba had already hung up. She switched off the phone and turned slowly toward the bed.

"Finally!" Maxine exclaimed.

"It was important, Max." Kate looked down at her, feeling uncomfortable without knowing why.

Come here, pretty woman," Maxine said, patting the mattress.

"Let's go, Max," Kate replied, a frown on her face. Kate was an alcoholic, but she no longer minded if people drank in her presence. What did bother her, though, was when they drank too much. She hated to see another woman go through her own private hell with the bottle. Kate had been lucky; after she had stopped drinking, she had only relapsed once — the night her last lover left her. But she had no illusions about the clinging power of booze; she knew that some women don't stop drinking until the day they die.

And being with a drunk was painfully reminiscent of her own past; she could see her reflection in every stupid, slurred remark, in every lopsided leer, in every uncontrolled, drunken flirtation with a total stranger she just had to have and whom she would inevitably hate as soon as she was sober, in every numb sexual encounter where her blood-alcohol level was probably higher than her sex drive, in every potential car crash, in every shameful, hung-over morning when she was forced to face the real world without the protection of her best friend, her worst enemy. All those wasted years, those one-night stands, those discarded lovers she might have liked had she ever got to know them, those pitiful orgasms, their intensity smothered in booze. Never again. No, never again. If life was painful, being drunk only made it worse. And alcohol couldn't end the pain; if she sometimes didn't know how to carry on, she was no different from thousands of other dykes struggling to maintain their identities in a world where every assumption was heterosexual.

"Aw, come on, don't be such a stick-in-the-mud. Come here and give me a little kiss," Maxine said, grinning.

She really is drunk, Kate realized with dismay.

"Come to mamma — " Maxine's hand snaked out and closed around Kate's wrist, and with surprising strength, she pulled Kate down beside her.

"Maxine, what are you doing?" Kate protested, trying to pull away. But Maxine was faster, pinning Kate to the bed and kissing her. The overpowering smell of alcohol was disgusting, making Kate gag.

"Stop it!"

"Come on, you want it as much as I do!"

Kate struggled to free herself, wincing with pain as Maxine's hands moved roughly over her body. "Maxine, don't!"

But Maxine wouldn't listen. She was breathing heavily, her eyes closed, her brows tightly knotted. Kate tried to hold her legs together when Maxine ripped open her slacks and forced her hand inside.

"Damn it! Open up, you bitch!"

Oh my god this can't really be happening, Kate thought numbly when Maxine's fist landed a sharp blow on the side of her face. Another woman wouldn't do this to me, *Maxine* wouldn't do this to me, she wouldn't, she couldn't. But she is, she is ... I'm being raped. Oh my god she's raping me and it hurts so bad ... "No, no, no," Kate whispered, the agony spreading.

"Jesus Christ, shut up!" Maxine said, giving Kate another clout on the cheek.

Kate sagged into the mattress, the stars which filled her eyes immediately replaced by tears of humiliation. Her senses were drowning in pain. She was being violated by a woman, a woman she had dated, trusted, laughed with, seriously considered loving. Oh Lord, how could this be? Was she crazy or had the world turned upside down?

Her whole being rebelled, and giving one massive shove, she dislodged Maxine and escaped from the bed, swaying on weak knees, pressing her hand against the wall for support. She felt woozy. Everything ached. There was blood on her sweater, on the front of her slacks. And she was incredibly angry. "Get out of my house!" Maxine rolled over to face her, her clothes dishevelled, her eyes bleary with drunkenness.

"Get out!"

"Wha — "

"You raped me!" Kate screamed. "Get out of my house!"

Maxine sat up slowly, looking confused. "I what?"

Kate stared at her, speechless. How could Maxine pretend that she didn't know what she had done?

"Aw, hon, I'm sorry I hit you. I just got a little carried away," Maxine said in a subdued, apologetic voice. "I had a little wine with dinner, and you've been putting me off for so long — "

"Get out, Maxine. If I never see you again it will be too soon," Kate said bitterly.

"Aw, don't be like that, Kate," Maxine cajoled, getting up.

"Don't come any closer," Kate warned, her hands balling into fists, ready to defend herself from another assault even though she was in such pain that she felt faint.

"Please, Kate, it'll never happen again," Maxine promised, reaching out to touch Kate on the shoulder.

Kate slapped her hand away, repulsed by her touch. "You can be damn certain it won't happen again," she said bitterly. "Now get out."

"Jesus, you'd think it was the end of the world," Maxine snarled, straightening her clothes and running fingers through her hair. "You'd think you never had sex before."

"That wasn't sex, Maxine. It was rape," Kate retorted, watching Maxine shrug into her coat.

"You've got to be kidding."

"I certainly am not," Kate responded at once.

"Jesus!" Maxine exclaimed, rolling her eyes. "Look, maybe I was a little rough, but rape? I mean, do you see any cocks around here?"

"Oh, just go," Kate said, disgust colouring her voice.

"You'll change your mind," Maxine blustered as she slipped into her gloves. "You'll want me back."

"Don't hold your breath." Or maybe she should, Kate thought hatefully. Maybe she should.

"Jesus. Women!"

Kate waited until she was sure Maxine was gone and then ran to the front door, shooting the bolt on the lock and fastening the chain. She walked through the house, drawing the blinds and turning on all the lights, and then returned to the bedroom and stripped, dropping her clothes directly into the hamper. She should throw them in the garbage; she would never be able to wear them again without being reminded of Maxine. But they were her best slacks, and they had cost a lot of money. And they weren't ripped. The blood would sponge off with cold water, and the zipper, which had come loose on one side, could easily be fixed with a needle and thread.

She slid her panties down over her hips, dismayed when she saw that the crotch was soaked with blood. She swiftly balled them up in her hands, went into the kitchen and stuffed them into the garbage bag under some banana peels and coffee grains. Some things were beyond salvage. She went back to the bedroom, trying not to worry about whether she was still bleeding. It had probably stopped, but if it hadn't, well, she would know soon enough.

Kate went into the bathroom and turned on the light. Her cheek was throbbing, her breasts sore, her nipples chapped. Her inner thighs felt bruised, and her vagina, oh, how to describe the pain in her poor, poor vagina!

She took a deep breath and looked at herself in the mirror, her knees wobbling at the sight of her swollen, raw-looking cheek. Tomorrow the bruises would deepen to colours no amount of make-up could camouflage, announcing to the world that something unspeakable had happened to her. No rare thing these days, she thought as the pale, scared and unforgettable faces of battered women waiting for treatment in the emergency room flitted before her eyes. But how would she explain to all her friends, lesbians for the most part, that another woman had done this to her? And what would she say at work? Were there a lot of battered nurses? A lot of raped nurses? If there were, why had she never heard about them? But what an idiotic question; if her first impulse was to hide the evidence, then so was everybody else's. She started the tub running, deliberating whether to add bath salts, deciding that it couldn't hurt. She soaked a facecloth in cold water and placed it gingerly against her aching cheek. And then the doorbell rang.

What if it was Maxine? Her heart thumped rapidly and she started to shiver. She turned off the taps, donned her bathrobe and tied it tightly around her. She walked stealthily through her flat to the door and gingerly placed her eye against the peep hole, expecting to see Maxine's drunken face on the other side. But it wasn't; it was Jo, an unlit cigarette dangling from her lips as she rocked impatiently on her heels.

Relief coursed through her veins; the shivering stopped. But what was she to do? How could she let Jo in? And if she did, what could she say? She hardly knew the young college student fidgeting in the cold outside her door. But the piercing ring of the doorbell made her decision for her; with all the lights on, how could she pretend that she wasn't home? She flipped the locks and opened the door.

"I know it's Saturday night and you're probably busy, you're probably getting ready to go out, but I've got to talk to you, maybe you'll think I'm crazy, I mean we don't know each other very well, but I haven't got anybody else and if I don't talk to somebody, I'm going to burst," Jo rambled. "And — hey! What happened to your face?"

"It's all right. Come in," Kate said.

"No, but I mean, your face — "

"I fell," Kate lied, turning away.

Jo reached out and gently removed the facecloth, paling as she stared at the swollen, abraded flesh. "Somebody hit you."

"I fell," Kate said firmly.

"Did somebody break in?" Jo asked, dropping her hand and staring around the apartment.

"No, no," Kate sighed tiredly, forcing her stiffening muscles to propel her body down the hall to the living room. All she wanted

**44**

was to soak away her misery and purify her unclean body in a hot bath and what she had on her hands was a hyperactive youngster needing to talk.

"You should call the police," Jo said, following Kate into the living room, perching attentively on the edge of a chair.

"No," Kate stated emphatically. The police? For a case of lesbian rape? Fat chance they would believe her. And if they did listen, it would probably be to get their rocks off.

"But he might come back," Jo said earnestly. "Did he — I mean, did he, ah, do anything else?"

"She," Kate replied with a sigh of resignation. "She. And yes she did."

Jo's eyes widened with disbelief and then dismay. "A woman?"

Why am I telling her this, Kate wondered. She's a stranger. And too young to be of any comfort. But she's here. Not Oats, who would be filled with the most satisfying righteous anger, not my mother, who would graciously but quite obviously forebear voicing her infuriatingly smug "I told you so" and lend me her shoulder to cry on, not anybody who can make a difference.

"Another woman hurt you like — like that?" Jo asked in a thin voice.

"Look, I really don't want to talk about it. So why don't you just tell me why you're here?"

Jo rapidly shook her head. "It doesn't matter. I thought it was important, but it isn't. Not now."

Kate stood up, weakness forcing her to grasp the back of the sofa to keep from falling.

"Here — let me help you." Jo put her arm around Kate's shoulder, and Kate sagged against the younger woman.

"I want to take a bath," Kate murmured. "I've got to get clean."

"I'll help," Jo assured her as they moved towards the bathroom together.

"I have to use the bathroom," Kate said.

"Sure."

Jo held her under the arms while she eased her body onto the toilet seat. Kate gasped with pain as acid urine burned her raw flesh. She closed her eyes, mortified that Jo was witnessing her suffering.

"Here's some toilet paper," Jo said in a matter-of-fact voice.

"Oh," Kate groaned. "I'm not sure I can get into the tub."

Jo untied her bathrobe and slid it from her, averting her eyes from Kate's body as she led her to the tub and over the side. "Here, sit down. I'll add more water."

Kate gingerly lowered herself to the rubber mat, groaning again as the warm water covered her bruised flesh. Would the pain never end?

"Do you want me to help you get washed?"

Kate forced her eyes open and looked up at Jo, who was standing indecisively with a facecloth and a bar of soap in her hand.

"No. I can manage," Kate responded, taking the cloth and the soap from her.

"Good. I'll go get some pyjamas."

"There's a nightie hanging on the back of the bedroom closet door," Kate told her.

"Okay."

As soon as she was alone Kate removed her glasses and put them on the toilet tank, and then set to work with the soap, lathering every part of her body, using the facecloth to scrub the dried blood from her inner thighs. She tentatively explored the tender spot between her legs, wincing as she gently tugged hardened pieces of blood from her pubic hair, then running the soap back and forth over her clitoris and the torn opening to her vagina. Would she ever feel clean again? She watched flakes of blood float to the top of the scummy water, and then reached down and pulled the plug, willing the evidence to disappear down the drain and her inner turmoil with it. How could Maxine have done this to her? And why hadn't she resisted, made her stop, hit back? Because she hadn't believed it was happening. Because she had been shocked to her very soul that another woman was capable of hitting her and forcing sex on her. Because lesbians didn't do that to each other. Except that Maxine had.

"Ready to come out? I've got a new towel, a nice, big soft one," Jo said, reappearing in the doorway with both her faded nightie and a large, thick beach towel. Any other time Kate would have been embarrassed about her old-fashioned, nearly floor-length, flannel nightie, but not now. She could hardly wait to put it on. Kate nodded mutely and reached up for the handle of the soap dish which was embedded in the tile.

"Need some help?"

She shook her head and stepped out of the tub, permitting Jo to wrap the towel snugly around her.

"There," Jo said, handing Kate her glasses.

Kate moved in slow-motion. Her anger was like a tight, coiled snake lying in wait in the pit of her stomach, but she felt too drained to make use of it. Never mind; it would still be there tomorrow. But what a dismal thought. She dropped the towel, past caring about her nudity. Jo helped her into her nightie and then led her to the bedroom. She had already drawn back the bedcovers, and Kate settled in bed with a sigh of relief. She felt Jo remove her glasses, and then sensed behind closed eyes that Jo was shutting the lights.

Moments later a second body eased itself under the covers, and for a second Kate tensed, drawing her back from that gracious, thoughtless state between sleep and awareness. "What — "

"Shhhh. Just sleep. I'll be here if you need me," Jo whispered. And when she reached out and gently drew Kate into her arms, Kate didn't resist. Seeking comfort, she pressed her face against Jo's breasts, and felt Jo's arms protectively curl around her. Lips brushed the top of her head just as she fell asleep.

# Change of Heart

**B**lue waited outside in the snowstorm, oblivious to the biting wind and the swirling, heavy snow which accumulated swiftly in the spikes of her hair and in the stiff creases of her leather jacket. She squinted up at the sombre brick walls of the women's residence, watching lights wink on and off in the large windows, staring as if concentrated wishing would magically force Jo to materialize in her room, or even better yet, there beside her.

Where the hell was she? It was nearly two in the morning and Jo was still out. Blue shoved her freezing, ungloved hands into her jacket pockets, picking absently at the ragged holes in the limp seems, enlarging them. She had been waiting since eleven for Jo to come home. She hadn't expected her to be gone when she had arrived, but the student working the reception desk had buzzed Jo's room repeatedly until she had succeeded in waking a groggy and obviously hungover Jock.

"She's not here," Jock had mumbled.

The receptionist had stared at her and Blue knew exactly what she was thinking. She had ignored her, trying to retain her dignity as she leaned over and asked, "do you know where she is?"

"Nope. She didn't say."

And that had been that. Three hours later and she was still waiting. Where could Jo be at two in the morning on a Saturday night? Blue had canvassed the bars, but nobody had seen her. Then again, who knows, maybe they had. Maybe Jo had gone off with another woman and nobody had wanted to tell her. Lesbians were just like other people: they didn't want to get involved when the news was bad. Some jilted dykes were just as likely to shoot the messenger as to thank her. And anyway, most of the lesbians she knew had enough problems of their own: unfaithful women, lovers not interested in sex, loneliness, a bruising case of the cruising blues. Not to mention problems at work, sick parents, kids who didn't listen, no money in their pockets or unsightly pimples. Besides, Jo at the bar was fair game, and lots of dykes would do anything to get their hands on a piece of fresh meat. Blue should know, since she had been one of them. And if there was anything she had learned in her relatively short life, it was that there was no question of loyalty when it came to sex.

She sighed, steeled her shoulders against the wind and let herself imagine the worst. Jo was angry, so she had probably gone off and done something stupid. Like purposefully picking up some horny desperado or having enough beers to get in the mood to tango between the sheets of some stranger's bed or finding herself an orgy in which to partake or or or ...

She kicked the snow, throttled her vivid imagination, called herself a few choice names and gave up on her vigil outside the women's residence. There was no sense in waiting for a lost cause to get worse. She would go back to the bar and have one last miserable beer. Or give Suzanne a call. Suzanne and her sidekick, madam dildo.

Naw. That was what had started the whole thing in the first place. That infamous Friday night at l'Entr'acte last fall when Jo was out of town and she had approached Suzanne, her ex-lover Karen's new lover. Out of curiosity, out of restlessness, out of rebellion, out of who knows what. Suzanne had initially been amused, but she had eventually responded, taking Blue home. Blue had been repulsed by the power games Suzanne played, but she had also been terribly excited, and the growing tendency to violence in their love-making had excited her even more, which was initially terrifying. She had loved it, she had hated it, she had grown ambivalent to the point of fascination. She had vowed never to return, but it had been a hollow vow, because she had gone back again and again, unable to stay away, wanting the kind of sex Suzanne offered and yet not wanting it, enchanted with submitting and yet despising the power Suzanne had over her. It was like a drug she had to have, the act itself some sort of undefined but rigorous archetype against which she had to measure herself.

She had cheated on Jo, but she didn't care about Suzanne. Maybe she even hated her, although it was hard to tell. It had started as a lark, a passing fancy, a sexual whim. Something new, something different. Nouveau sleaze or a real twentieth century lesbian screw, depending on your point of view. How could she have known that it would continue throughout the long, cold winter, like a fire smouldering under the ground long after the flame has been extinguished? It was done with mirrors, it was the result of the worst kind of shameless, insincere flattery, it was bogus, meaningless tripe. Or perhaps it was simply postmodern sex. Still, Blue had tried it, and it hadn't fit. She didn't really want it, postmodern or not, but since it was there, it had proved impossible to resist. Perhaps that was the punk in her. That was what she chose to believe, refusing to regress to an archaic interpretation which would force her to reclassify herself. It had nothing to do with that — she was her own woman, after all. But Jo's reaction had been catastrophic, leaving Blue straddled between two worlds. She had been boxed in, forced to reevaluate. If she wasn't careful, she was going to lose interest in sex.

So no, she couldn't go to Suzanne's. The delicious ambiguity of the increasingly violent sex games Suzanne enticed her into playing wasn't enough to propel her in that direction. Even the possibility that this time she might enjoy herself without the attendant feelings of self-betrayal and the lingering angst she suffered for days on end couldn't motivate her to face the knowing gleam in Suzanne's eyes or the amused expression on Karen's face. Perhaps Suzanne's mild sadism, Karen's blatant voyeurism and Blue's growing masochistic responses weren't intrinsically humiliating, but Blue felt humiliated anyway. Maybe Suzanne wanted to dominate her because Blue had been Karen's lover. Or maybe Suzanne just got her kicks from dominating other women. It didn't have to be complicated to be true. But enough. If she didn't like it, she wasn't going to do it any more. Yeah, sure, she thought cynically, shivering from the cold as she opened the heavy metal door to the subway. I wonder how long I'll keep that particular resolution.

"Blue! Hey, Blue! Wait up!"

Oh no. Not that nerd. That was all she needed to end this miserable evening.

"I saw you from the window," Jock puffed, "and thought you might want to go for a beer."

Blue looked at Jock's hope-filled, cold-reddened face and sighed. "Sure. Why not? I guess l'Entr'acte is still open."

Jock's grin was so genuine and so innocent that Blue found herself grinning back in spite of herself. "Let's go, then. They're going to close in less than an hour."

They set out in the direction of the bar, their shoulders hunched to keep out the penetrating wind. L'Entr'acte was nearly deserted; there was never much action that late at night. Couples were already home in bed sleeping the satiated sleep of the already-mated, and those who had successfully cruised were in bed but definitely not wasting time sleeping. Instead, they were frantically toiling to make their dreams come true or to at least procure a decent orgasm from a perfect stranger. Singles who had grown lonelier with each successive beer were now safely tucked behind closed doors, and, too horny or too depressed or too drunk to masturbate, they were licking their wounds with one last lung-torturing cigarette or one final numbing drink.

Loud dance music filled the empty spaces between the exposed, crumbling brick walls, but no one was dancing. Women sagged over their beer bottles, exhausted by the night's action or lack thereof. Blue tossed her jacket on a stool, ordered a beer and fed quarters into the insatiable maw of the flashing jukebox.

"Do you want to dance?" Jock asked, hovering over her shoulder, her beer bottle dangling from one hand.

"Naw. I'm just putting on some slow songs so we can hear ourselves think," Blue replied. She sipped her beer and took a look at Jock, suddenly wary. Was Jock was intending to come on to her? Un-uh, no way. Disaster city writ large. She wasn't even attracted to her, although it wouldn't be the first time she had surrendered to proximity, to one of those spur-of-the-moment things she had usually regretted before it was over. Some uncharted territories were better left unexplored, and this was certainly one of them. "Let's sit down," she said, turning abruptly and walking swiftly to a table at the front of the bar where the loud music was partially muted.

"So … " Jock began, taking a nervous swig from her beer bottle.

"Yeah?"

"So here we are," Jock said, clumsily lighting a cigarette.

Blue stifled a grin and nodded instead.

"You and Jo had a fight."

"I don't particularly want to talk about that."

"Oh. Sorry."

Silence ensued. Jock finished her cigarette, stabbed it out, and then began peeling the label from her beer bottle, heaping soggy slips of paper in a messy pile on the table. "See, I met this woman at Ruff, and I think she was coming on to me."

So now it's time for true confessions, Blue thought with dismay. Didn't she have enough trouble in her own life without adding this little one's adolescent misery to it?

"Her name is Candy. Do you know her?"

Candy, the bombshell of the pool tables. Who will play any game you want, you only have to ask. Slut might be the correct descriptive term. But she would be charitable, and anyway, slut was probably too strong a term to use to describe somebody she had slept with. "Yeah. We've met," Blue replied laconically. In the carnal sense, especially, but that was last year, so it doesn't mean anything now. Ancient history, and therefore irrelevant, especially to a virgin like Jock.

"I don't know how to tell if she was coming on to me," Jock confessed. "I mean, we were playing pool and then she came over to the bar and asked for my phone number."

Boy, this was ignorance personified; what woman would go to the trouble of asking for a phone number and then never use it? Especially if the woman in question was Candy. "So has she called you?"

"Not yet," Jock said despondently.

"Well, don't give up hope." Candy was probably busy; she would get around to Jock when she grew tired of her current lover. Candy believed in having somebody in reserve to create a sense of security, however false it inevitably was. No matter how bored she became, Candy never dismissed one lover until she had a replacement hovering in the wings. She despised cold sheets, and she was overly fond of an appreciative presence in her bed after the main bout was over. Perhaps she was still into having a multitude of partners, although she had sworn to Blue that those days were over, not because of moral reservations or because she had the HIV jitters, but because it was simply too complicated to keep her lovers in separate compartments and to remember whose name to cry out at the appropriate moment.

"Maybe I should call her," Jock said. "What do you think?"

Blue shrugged. Advice to the love-lorn was not her strong point, especially since she didn't even seem to be capable of managing her own love life lately.

"I don't have her number anyway," Jock concluded glumly.

Blue juggled her nearly empty beer bottle and looked at Jock. They were close in age, but in terms of experience, she could have been Jock's grandmother. What did Jock want her to say? There was no magic formula for success between the sheets, just as there were no pithy truths which could simplify love. If you wanted sex badly enough, you could get it practically anywhere. But love, well, that was another matter entirely. And anyway, what was love? Jo thought she was in love with her, but how did she know? How did anybody know? Maybe it was just infatuation, hormones or simply a way to escape solitary confinement. Who needed it? It always complicated life. Why couldn't Jo let things be? Why did she need to define everything? Blue didn't like jealous women. She didn't want to be owned. She was punk because she was a free spirit. Whatever that means, she thought wryly, remembering her last night with Suzanne. Maybe even free spirits have their limits, although though they don't particularly want to admit it …

"Want another beer?"

Blue nodded absently, lost in thought. She had tried to keep her distance from Jo, but Jo had jumped in feet first, falling in love without getting to know Blue first, without worrying about whether Blue would fall in love too. It had been difficult to remain detached when Jo was so affectionate, so loving, so sexy. Ah yes, the sex. For a sexual neophyte, Jo was a marvellous lover. She was passionate and inventive, and she made Blue feel good in bed.

Yeah, that and fifty cents might get you a case of heartache, Blue thought sourly, looking at Jock as she deposited two bottles of beer on the table.

"We've only got ten minutes, so drink up," Jock said despondently, a half-smoked cigarette pressed between two fingers.

"No problem," Blue replied, raising the bottle to her lips and chug-a-lugging, spurred on by Jock's appreciative grin. She felt the beer hit her empty stomach, warm her extremities, kill a few unsuspecting brain cells and numb the rest.

"So you don't know where Jo went, huh?" she asked, carefully setting her empty bottle on the table in front of her.

"She was really upset. I think she went to visit somebody, but I don't know who," Jock replied.

"It doesn't matter." Where would Jo go? She didn't know that many women, not yet. Maybe she went back to her first lover for a little comfort, some commiseration, a bit of revenge.

"Closing time," the bartender shouted.

Jock stood up, stretched, and shrugged into her coat. "You can come back to the dorm with me and wait," she suggested hopefully. And let Jo know that she was upset? No way. "Thanks but no thanks. I've got to get my beauty sleep," Blue replied lightly, sweeping a hand through her spikes to straighten them.

"I wish," Jock laughed.

Candy didn't deserve the honour of initiating this nice young thing, Blue mused as she zipped up her jacket. Yeah, just like she didn't deserve the mess she was in. "Tell Jo I'll call her."

"Sure."

The streets were deserted. It had stopped snowing, and their boot-prints marred the unbroken expanse of virgin snow covering the sidewalk. It was dazzlingly white, sparkling even under the dim illumination of the high street lamps evenly spaced along St-Denis Street. By tomorrow it would be dingy, much of it reduced to slush by the daytime traffic. The wind stirred, and clumps of snow fell from the trees like clots of blood from a recent wound. Blue stared up at the sky. It was a sickening shade of yellow, reflecting the never-extinguished lights of the city. I feel like that looks, she thought. What if I am in love with Jo? Can you be in love and not know it?

"So here's where I turn off," Jock said. "Sure you won't come back with me? She's got to be home by now."

"Next time."

"Well, see you, then."

Blue managed a smile. "Have a good night."

"You too."

The subway was closed, and the buses were infrequent this late at night. Blue didn't have money for a cab, so she decided to walk. Maybe exercise would clear the confusion from her mind. For a free-spirited punk, she was awfully earth-bound, and she didn't much like the feeling.

# No More Words

Oats felt like a rusted-out car abandoned by the side of the road, the windshields long ago shattered into pointed slivers now haphazardly decorating the sprung, mildewed seats, thick spears of grass aggressively poking through jagged holes in the deteriorating floor. She sighed with unaccustomed tiredness, pulled herself into a sitting position and stared out the window, watching the wind whip falling snow into a maelstrom. She felt depressed; if she had had the energy she would have cried, but her tear ducts seemed inoperable. Anyway, there was far too much snow this winter; no sooner had one snowstorm ended than another had spread its white fire across the city skies, snarling traffic, indiscriminately covering the roofs of rich and poor alike. No discrimination there, although the poor couldn't rely on airtight windows, adequate insulation or efficient heating systems to keep them warm on cold winter nights. But oh, the snow. Tons and tons of the damn stuff. That was why this inexplicable thing, this stupid heart attack, had taken her down. Maybe global warming was a figment of somebody's imagination. Maybe all these blizzards were a harbinger of the end of the world. Maybe there would be a new ice age; it would never stop snowing and there would be snow piled high on the ground next July, with a diminished sun shining wanly in the pale sky. Maybe the earth was truly and finally finished. Just like her.

She cautiously wiggled her behind, trying to find a more comfortable position. Like Humpty Dumpty, she had disintegrated into a thousand pieces, and she didn't know how to put herself together again. Heart, lungs, muscles, skin, arms and legs, fingers and toes, mind and soul — everything was adrift and searching for home. But it was all in vain, because home wasn't there any more, not since she had passed out in agony and fallen senselessly to earth like a lump of packed snow. She hadn't felt comfortable in her body since then. She had been betrayed and the trust was gone, like when a love affair goes wrong. She was as weak as a baby, her muscles flaccid, her thoughts distorted with fear and confusion. Yes, she was afraid. Afraid that there would be more pain, afraid of dying, afraid she would live to be an invalid. During the day the hospital routine distracted her, but at night, terror reigned. Fear dominated her dreams, punctuating them with frustrating games of hide-and-seek where nothing was ever found, with mocking laughter and false tears, with endings but no beginnings.

The day she was released from intensive care and left most of her IV lines and the oxygen tent behind, they sent a recovered heart attack patient to visit her. The hospitals were big on self-help groups, perhaps because it enabled them to discharge patients faster. And now that she was out of immediate danger, it was time for a pep talk. Oh sure, she knew that they were just trying to reassure her that she had a life ahead of her, but what kind of life was it going to be? No more playing the role of the wild woman, ready for any adventure. No more cruising headlong into the unknown. No more cigarettes, booze, junk food, partying the night away. Lots of rest, exercise, vegetables. Early to bed, early to rise. She was certain that death couldn't be much more boring than a life like that.

The woman had been thin, vivacious and rosy-cheeked under her skilfully applied make-up, and, of course, straight. Oats despised her on sight. With her tiny, flat breasts and narrow hips, she had the look of a teenager seriously flirting with anorexia. Oats liked women with a little meat on their bones, and she certainly couldn't imagine herself ever being that skinny. She would lose something of her identity if she lost that much weight, because as far as she was concerned, butches were supposed to be imposing in stature. The skinny butches Oats knew were all young; give them a couple of decades, and they would grow horizontally. Except for the punk butches. Nobody knew how they would grow. And nobody cared, either, except for the punk femmes. Maybe. It was hard to know whether punks thought about that kind of stuff, and even harder to know if they cared. Anyway, this lady had chatted on and on about exercise and dieting with the enthusiasm of a recently converted twelve-stepper. Kate had been like that once, just after she had discovered Alcoholics Anonymous and got sober, but Oats had simply ignored it until Kate was sufficiently recovered to realize that there was still a world out there. But this straight woman was another matter — it seemed to Oats that concern about diet and health and avoiding another heart attack had become her whole life, and that it was going to stay that way forever. It had been hard to concentrate, and even harder to care about what she was saying. Toward the end of her visit, she had whispered in an intimate, confidential aside that sex with her husband was better now that she had lost weight and was in good shape. Her husband seemed to like her that way, she had mumbled, her cheeks growing even redder. As if Oats cared. As if being attractive to her man was an issue. As if her world turned in the same direction.

Oats had listened because she didn't have any other choice. She had been a captive audience of one, tied to her bed by both weakness and various plastic tubes feeding copious amounts of medication into her body. And in reality, she didn't have anything better to do; she had lost interest in TV, she wasn't able to concentrate on reading the tattered women's magazines Kate had brought from the visitor's room, and she had grown tired of watching the falling snow kiss the window before it moved on. One snowflake was pretty much like another, and so were the TV shows and magazines. So she had listened, willing herself to be generous and open-minded, but nothing the woman said had touched her. The words had been right, but the messenger was wrong. Oats knew about heartache, not heart disease; that hadn't been an issue in the lesbian community. Straight people had heart attacks, especially type-A, emotionally constipated men. But dykes? She'd never heard of a lesbian having a heart attack. Crotch rot, yes, even an embarrassing case of VD once in a while, and certainly breast cancer, which happened with such depressing regularity that it was more like a lesbian plague than anything else, but a heart attack?

The thought of modelling herself after that chirpy little straight gal made her want to laugh, although laughing was yet another thing which was now out of the question, since it made her heart beat faster. She had never been so conscious of that fragile organ thumping inside her chest. Sometimes she felt her pulse, holding her breath when it slowed down or speeded up, wondering if her heart was about to explode, implode or simply stop. She had asked, but they couldn't tell her whether it would happen again. All they said was that she was less likely to have another heart attack if she "changed her lifestyle." Well, what the hell was that supposed to mean? And what was wrong with the way she had been living her life, anyway?

Oats slid down under the covers, pulling them up to her neck. She was tired of looking at the snow. It was always white. It either fell straight down or blew around long enough to stick to things or blossom into irregularly shaped snowbanks which always grew the highest just where you had to cross the street. She was even more tired of rehashing her suddenly incipient mortality over and over again. She hated being sick. She hated being an invalid. She hated her body for doing this to her.

"Kind of boring, huh?" commented her roommate, a woman of uncertain age who persisted in making conversation despite Oats' blatant display of disinterest.

"Yeah."

"Maybe they'll serve us lunch soon."

Maybe? Lunch always came at noon sharp; you could set your watch on it. "Yeah."

"When are you getting out?"

"Who knows?"

"My doctor said I could leave tomorrow," her roommate informed her. "My husband is going to come and get me after lunch."

"Good for you," Oats replied. And for me, she mused. Although with my luck, they'll probably wheel in somebody who snores like a chainsaw or a post-op patient who will moan all night long. Or another woman intent on making her roommate into a life-long friend. She decided she'd rather have the snorer, even the moaner.

Oats tugged at her covers, pulling them over her head. "I think I'll get some sleep."

"That's good, dear. Rest is the best medicine."

Oats sighed and closed her eyes. She felt so lonely. How did other dykes manage when they got sick? Did they pine away in isolation in hospitals like she was doing, their lesbianism unnoted on their charts, their identity unrecognized by doctors, nurses, roommates? That stupid resident, asking her what method of birth control she used, as if all women automatically needed to. And the woman who had filled out that interminably long form, her plucked eyebrows arching in a clear statement of disapproval when Oats had answered "no" to all her questions about marital status, children and all the other accoutrements of heterosexuality. No, she was not married. Not divorced. Not separated. Not widowed. Not living common law. Not pregnant and never had been. Not on the pill. Had never used a diaphragm. Et cetera. You would think that they had never seen a dyke before. Heterosexuals were so smug, so thoughtlessly certain that everybody else was like them. As if the only natural place for a penis was in a vagina. Heaven help the woman who wanted to keep her vagina to herself, or preferred to get off another way; she was either irrelevant, threatening or immoral.

Oats tugged on her sheet, trying to stretch out the creases. Whether it was being done automatically, without forethought or malice, or whether it was being done on purpose, they were trying to make her invisible. And of course they were succeeding. She felt cut loose from life, isolated from everything familiar. It would have been better to fade away at home than to endure this festering alienation. She hadn't felt so adrift since she was twelve and her breasts had suddenly grown sore and sprouted, their tiny presence driving a permanent wedge between her and the boys in the neighbourhood. Suddenly, she had no frame of reference. She was a girl, one of those horrible others, and they didn't want to play with her any more. In a sense, life had been like that ever since; heteros still wouldn't play with you unless it was their game with their rules.

"Sue? Are you awake?"

Oats reluctantly removed the sheet from her face and gave Melba a wan grin. "Hi, there."

"Hi."

"How are you?"

"I should be the one asking that question," Melba said with a distant smile.

"It's about time you got some company besides that nurse who's always coming around," commented her roommate.

Oats grimaced at Melba, who looked amused. "Why don't you pull the curtain?" she suggested.

Not that it would make much difference, Oats mused, watching Melba tug at the curtain. Its thin fabric wouldn't create much more than a psychological barrier between them and Oats' inquisitive roommate.

"There's a chair down there."

"I can't stay long," Melba warned her, but she moved the chair to the side of the bed and sat down.

Oats wanted to reach out and touch Melba, to see if she still felt the same, but Melba had positioned herself out of reach, and not just physically. "So," Oats began, clearing her throat nervously. "How are you?"

"Inconsiderate if not downright cruel and thoughtless," Melba replied. "According to your friends, that is."

"Oh." Oats suddenly wanted a cigarette. Her longing was so fierce that she could almost taste it and feel the pungent aroma of burning tobacco curling around her nostrils, the sharpness of the smoke in her lungs.

"I felt guilty, so here I am," Melba added.

"Well, we wouldn't want that, would we?" Oats said bitterly, turning away.

"Oh, don't act so wounded, so innocent," Melba shot back. "I suppose next thing you'll start blaming me for having a heart attack."

"No," Oats said slowly. "No, I'd never do that." She gathered courage from the silence which followed and glanced at Melba, astonished to see tears running down her cheeks. Damn it, she thought. Just damn it. "Look, I'm sorry."

Melba shook her head and impatiently wiped away the tears. "Don't you see, I don't want your apologies. You can't undo what you've done."

Well then, what could she do? Nothing. Just a big flat nothing. She had been dumber than dumb, and all for a fleeting piece of tail. "You're better off without me," she mumbled. She wasn't of any use to anybody any more, not even herself. Who would want her? Not Melba, not after what she had done. And certainly not any playmates she had so casually dated, slept with and then just as thoughtlessly discarded when the next opportunity came along. None of them would want her, not now that she was damaged goods.

"Of course I'd be better off without you," Melba responded vehemently. "Don't you think I knew that right from the beginning?"

"Oh."

"Yes, oh."

"My reputation preceded me, did it?"

"Don't sound so smug about it," Melba said hotly. "Although I imagine you can't help yourself."

"Sorry."

"And stop being so damn humble. It doesn't suit you."

Oats sighed. Why had Melba bothered to come if all she was going to do was pick to pieces everything Oats said? "So did your sister have her baby?" she asked, grasping at straws, desperate to normalize the conversation.

Melba nodded. "She had a girl. Eight pounds six ounces. Her name is Melodie."

"Congratulations! I bet you're pleased." Oats tried to put a little enthusiasm in her voice, but she sounded as animated as a flat line on one of those heart machines she had been hooked up to.

"Sue, what on earth is the matter with you?" Melba asked impatiently. "Get a grip on yourself!"

Which "yourself" was Melba referring to? The Oats who made hay while the sun shined, claiming permanent ownership to at least one bar stool in every lezzie bar in the city, swilling beer down her perpetually dry gullet while spouting romantic platitudes to any cute thing willing to listen, not counting the evening a success until she had a willing partner in her bed? The Oats who considered variety the spice of life, who liked her women to be mysterious, who thought seduction was a galactic imperative? Or the hidden, thoughtful Oats who had responded to Melba's strengths, to her belief that attraction was the beginning of something rather than an end in itself, to her coupling of sex with the growth of love and commitment?

"I see you've had time to think," Melba said gently.

"Lots," Oats responded somewhat dryly. About life and death and other heavy stuff which she had previously avoided like the plague. Since her heart attack, she had spent altogether too much time listening to the chaos of her inner bodily rhythms and waxing uncharacteristically pensive. There had been so many morbid thoughts that the growth of fatalism had been inevitable, a normal (or so she supposed) response to the shocking loss of control over her life. In other words, she had temporarily misplaced her spunk. "I thought about us a lot," she added. And that wasn't a lie, not really; when she hadn't been obsessed with dying, she had been obsessed with Melba.

"And what do you think?"

"That I was a fool," Oats answered honestly.

"And how long did it take you to realize that?" Melba asked, rising from her chair and walking to the window. Oats followed her with her eyes, then looked past her to the thick flakes of snow spiralling down. They were seeing the same thing; snow falling innocently from the sky, its direction dictated by the capricious wind. It could have been romantic. It could have sparked a reconciliation between them. Well, it could have made *some* difference, anyway. If she could have slipped out of bed and managed to stand on legs which hadn't supported her weight for far too long. If she could have put her arm around Melba's shoulder. If Melba would have let her. Too many ifs when even one was enough to make romance disappear as fast as a rabbit in a magician's act. Or as swiftly as money at the race track. Or a beer in a bar.

"I knew it before I had the heart attack," Oats replied.

"I was very hurt."

"I know."

"I didn't want to come here, Sue," Melba said. "When I left that morning, I promised myself I'd never look back. It was over."

"I know." With a growing sense of finality, Oats realized that there was nothing she could say which would make a difference. When Melba had discovered Frédérique's steamy little love letter and a sexually sated Oats sprawled nearly comatose in a decidedly sex-scented bed, it had already been too late for words. The deed was definitely done. Oats' selfish actions had effectively destroyed their still-fragile relationship, had nipped trust at the bud before it had had the opportunity to fully bloom.

"I don't know why I always end up getting hurt," Melba mused, her nose nearly touching the windowpane. "I guess I have this bad habit of falling for the wrong women."

"But I've changed, Melba," Oats blurted, wanting to convince her that she wasn't one of those wrong women. Sleeping with Frédérique had been a mistake, and she would never do it again. She knew better now. "I've learned my lesson."

"And what lesson is that?" Melba asked immediately, turning away from the snowstorm to face Oats. "That you can't lie, that you can't be unfaithful when you've promised to work on a relationship? Or that the next time you get the itch, you'll make sure you don't get caught?"

Oats turned away from Melba's anger, her strength depleted, her meagre reserve of emotional energy sapped. If only they had had this conversation before her heart attack. Everything was too mixed up now. Hell, she was too mixed up now. "I've changed, Melba," she repeated, unable to say more.

"Oh, tell me another one," Melba said scornfully. "Tell me something I haven't heard before. Something I can believe."

"You're not making this any easier," Oats responded with a spark of anger.

"Why should I?"

Because Oats loved her. Because she didn't want to lose her for good. Tears welled up in her eyes; this was altogether too much. Melba was not going to forgive her, and what was worse, for the first time ever, she was finding it hard to forgive herself. It was devastating.

"Oh god, don't *you* cry!" Melba exclaimed.

Oats covered her face with her hands to hide the streaming tears. "I can't help it."

Melba's soft, thin hands touched hers, then gently pried them away. She lifted Oats' head, forcing Oats to look up. A corner of Melba's mouth lifted in a slight, one-sided smile. "You look so miserable."

Oats wrenched her head away, hating her vulnerability. She had always pretended to be strong, invincible. Getting emotional in front of somebody else, especially a lover, was a fatal error, bad for her image. But what a laugh; the old days were irretrievably gone. Her image was in tatters, and there wasn't a damn thing she could do about it.

"This is the first time I've seen you do something really genuine," Melba whispered, grasping Oats' head and turning it. "Except for coming, of course." Her face was so close that Oats could see the fine lines around her mouth and in the corner of her eyes. And then, incredibly, Melba kissed her. Not a soft, questioning kiss but a possessive taking, Melba's familiar tongue slipping between her chapped lips, reaching as if to reclaim something lost. Oats felt no passion; instead, her whole being ached with loss.

"It was either that, or spank you," Melba said, pulling away abruptly.

"I love you," Oats whispered desperately, and this belated confession made her start crying again.

"I know," Melba said, and then she left the room.

# Taking Liberties

"**B**lue was here last night," Jock said. She was lying flat on her back on her narrow bed, her thighs slack, her bare toes pointing in opposite directions.

"Why didn't you tell me?" Jo responded, wrenching her thoughts away from Kate. The impact of Blue's betrayal had faded after she had inadvertently stumbled into Kate's private hell. Immobilized in an uncomfortable position because Kate's arms had been wrapped around her in a passionless embrace, she had been unable to sleep, although Kate had drifted sporadically into short, nightmare-filled dozes, waking with a jolt every so often. They hadn't talked much even when Kate was awake; Jo was afraid that she would say something wrong and break the fragile connection between them, a paper-thin bond born of Kate's desperate need to hold on to someone, anyone, and Jo's stunned willingness to respond to it.

"How could I? You just got home a couple of minutes ago, and I didn't even know where you were. And anyway, where were you? Why won't you tell me?" Jock asked plaintively.

Jo flopped back on her bed with a groan. "Because it's confidential, that's why. I promised." Jock was shameless; she would swear on a stack of bibles that she would keep a secret and then proceed to blurt everything to Tony. And Tony was the champion blabbermouth of the world, shamelessly using information to gain popularity. "Anyway, how was Blue?"

"I don't know. Grumpy, I guess."

"Was she upset that I wasn't here?"

"Well, she wasn't pleased," Jock replied with a rare exhibition of wryness.

"You're being helpful," Jo commented.

"Look, she doesn't confide in me," Jock responded, sitting up and looking over at Jo. "I don't even think she likes me."

Jo shrugged, feeling uncomfortable. It wasn't that Blue actually disliked Jock, she just thought that Jock was incredibly immature. And naive. Blue didn't have much use for women who didn't know which way was up. Or who were virgins. Not that it was Jock's fault, although sometimes even Jo felt impatient with her, because really, with so many available women around, why hadn't Jock stumbled over one who was attracted to her? Jo herself had been cruised so many times that she had lost count, and sometimes she had been strongly tempted. But no. She had been dutifully faithful while Blue had gone on her merry, cheating way. And doing it with a dildo, yet! Jo shivered, wondering if all her illusions were fated to be shattered before the end of her first year in university. Lesbians raping other lesbians, lesbians hitting other lesbians, lesbians using dildos — was this commonplace or had she simply crossed paths with a bunch of weirdos? Was this a really how sophisticated, big-city lesbians behaved? If so, maybe she should have listened to her parents and attended a small town college!

"See? Even you think that Blue doesn't like me," Jock complained, smashing her cigarette butt in the overflowing ashtray and staring agitatedly at Jo.

"I said no such thing," Jo retorted, interrupting Jock's litany of woes. "She doesn't know you, that's all."

"Yeah, and she doesn't care to, either," Jock blustered, turning away from Jo and lighting another cigarette.

So some people like you and some don't, Jo thought tiredly; that's life, kiddo. And it works both ways, too.

"Where were you last night?" Jock said, stubbornly refusing to let it go, much to Jo's annoyance.

"You'll never know," Jo replied lightly. Okay, so maybe she was being just a little bit tough on her best friend, but enough was enough. It was time for Jock to grow up, to realize that she wasn't always going to get what she wanted. She could do her damnedest and still get the exact opposite — that is, if she even got anything at all. Yeah, and who are we talking about here, Jo thought with a wry chuckle. It sure as hell ain't Jock.

"I bet you were out screwing around," Jock said.

"And so what if I was?"

"But Blue — "

"Blue has been out there doing a little screwing around herself," Jo interrupted. This was probably a mistake, but she had to tell someone or burst, and while lovers might grow on trees, friends sure didn't.

"You're kidding!" This made Jock sit up and take notice, as Jo had known it would.

"I wish. Give me a cigarette."

Jock got up and walked over to Jo's bed. "You shouldn't smoke," she said.

"Look who's talking," Jo retorted, taking a cigarette from the pack.

"Yeah, right," Jock said with a laugh. She sat down and lit Jo's cigarette. "Anyway, Jo, I didn't know about Blue. I knew you suspected something, but I didn't realize you'd found out that it was true. I'm sorry."

"That's life," Jo shrugged.

"Did you break up with her?" Jock asked, lighting another cigarette for herself.

"I don't know."

"What do you mean, you don't know?"

"Just that. We argued, and she left. Neither of us said anything about breaking up," Jo explained.

"Are you still in love with her?"

If she wasn't in love, she wouldn't care what Blue did in her spare time. But she felt wary now, although not about what Jock would tell Tony. Jock cared; she wouldn't do anything to hurt her, not intentionally, anyway. But something had changed; witnessing Kate's agony had tempered her thoughts and feelings with a new cautiousness. From the time she had been little, life had always seemed like a game, one she had been able to play without effort. There had been more victories than defeats, and none of the defeats had touched her deeply. But if life really was just a game, then some people got badly hurt playing it, like Kate. And maybe it wasn't a game. Maybe it was something altogether different. You were born, you grew up the best way you could, made choices about how you were going to live your life, who you were going to love, what you were going to do, all without knowing if you were right. Nobody ever had enough information. All you had going for you were the instincts you were born with and all those contradictory things you learned from the people around you, from books, from living. The consequences of your choices were sometimes positive, sometimes deadly, and it was often impossible to know the difference. And sometimes things happened without reason, randomly. Like being killed in a car crash. Or having a heart attack, like Oats. Or being beaten up and raped by your girlfriend.

"Sorry. I guess I shouldn't have asked," Jock muttered.

"What?"

"I shouldn't have asked if you were still in love with her," Jock explained, looking away.

Jo put out her cigarette and sat up, slumping against her roommate's side. "Oh, Jock. How did I get myself into this mess?"

"It's not your fault," Jock said stolidly.

"You would say that," Jo said with weary amusement, ignoring the fact that Jock had put her arm around her shoulder. Jock was as loyal as a puppy dog and almost as transparent, but still, it was surprising how good it felt to snuggle up to her warm, solid body. She could feel Jock's tension, her minute trembling. Her housecoat had come undone, exposing her small, round-shaped breasts with their surprisingly large, dusky nipples. Jo was tempted to reach out and cup one of them in her hand, to feel the nipple harden perceptibly in her palm. What naughty thoughts she was having; she wasn't in love with Jock, and it wouldn't be fair to lead her on. Still …

"It isn't your fault that Blue's been acting like a bitch," Jock said vehemently, tightening her grasp on Jo's shoulder.

"Jock, you're just so dependable," Jo said, slipping her hand inside Jock's housecoat and hugging her. This growing urge to seduce her lifelong friend was insane. She had never, ever been attracted to Jock, had never even felt a momentary buzz of desire. But it was so gratifying to feel Jock's flesh turn to butter the second she touched her. "I shouldn't be doing this," she whispered, taking Jock's taut nipple between her fingers.

"Neither should I," Jock said breathlessly as her hands fumbled in their eagerness to open the tiny buttons of Jo's nightgown.

"Then let's not."

"Oh, no — " Jock protested as Jo's hands fell away. "Please!"

"It's not fair, Jock." Jo moved away and lit a cigarette.

"Fair? Fair? What do you mean, fair?" Jock sputtered.

"I don't love you."

"I know. I've always known. But it doesn't matter."

"It does to me."

"Jo, please … "

Something in Jock's voice touched her. Their eyes met, Jo's full of uncertainly, Jock's brimming over with need, with an almost pitiful pleading. It was tempting, but it was wrong. She would be no better than Blue if she let it happen. But happen it would, she realized, watching Jock throw off her housecoat, exposing her broad, still-tanned shoulders, her paler breasts, their nipples already taut, her flat belly. And she was going to let it happen whether it was right or wrong, she realized further as Jock lifted Jo's nightgown over her head, moaning when her body came into view. And even participate in its happening, she thought suddenly as Jock moved over her. And then, as their bodies came together and touched, she stopped thinking altogether, reaching up to hold her, parting her lips for Jock's kiss, which, when it came, was so explosive that she knew she had been fooling herself. She wanted Jock, all of her, regardless of the consequences, in spite of Blue, and whether she was in love with Jock or not. If that made her guilty as sin, more despicable than Blue, then so be it.

"I love you," Jock whispered, and Jo felt her hands move tentatively from her breasts to the tangle of soft pubic hair below the rise of her belly.

"Shhhh."

Passion held and then intensified, enabling Jo to swallow her guilt. She opened her thighs and raised her hips, encouraging Jock to slide her fingers over her hot, creamy flesh, to explore her swollen clit and move lower. She reached between Jock's legs, pausing to stroke the silky skin on her inner thighs before she began to rub her clit. Jock came almost at once, and Jo imagined she could feel a lifetime of repressed desire exploding in that one orgasm.

"Oh god!"

"Shhh," Jo whispered, reaching down and moving Jock's hand, showing how she wanted it, concentrating on her own orgasm. It was elusive; she would reach the brink and then lose it, slowing her movements to let it rebuild. She toyed with Jock's clit, feeling how sopping wet she was. Jock was breathing heavily, sweat gathering on her back and between her breasts, her hard-tipped nipples scraping Jo's chest as she moved over her.

"This is so good," Jock said, her voice husky.

"Yes, like that!" Jo exclaimed, pushing up, forcing Jock's fingers deep inside. "Move, move!"

Jo felt Jock obey, thrusting her fingers in and out of her vagina, and she moaned quietly, coming hard, hugging Jock to her, pressing her breasts into her chest. She was incredibly hungry, and her orgasm lasted for a long time. Imagine Jock being such a butch, she thought absently as Jock's fingers coaxed the last few flutters from her vagina. Just imagine. And then it was over; her vagina relaxed, closing around Jock's still fingers.

"You're heavy," Jo said with a short laugh.

Jock moved immediately. "Sorry."

Jo rose to a sitting position and straightened her hair. "How about a cigarette?"

"Sure."

She watched Jock light two cigarettes, then took one from her. "Jock — "

"I know. It doesn't mean anything," Jock said with a vicious drag on her cigarette.

"That's not what I was going to say," Jo replied. "Of course it meant something."

"But it doesn't *change* anything." Another agitated drag on the cigarette, which by now had an enormous red tip.

Jo bent down and picked up her nightgown from the floor, slipping it over her head. What a colossal mistake this had been. Why hadn't she listened to those early warning signals instead of indulging herself and surrendering to Jock's desperate need? "Don't look at me like that," she said with a long sigh, reaching out and gathering up Jock's broader hands in her own. "I don't want you to feel like this."

Jock shrugged uncomfortably and looked away.

"Look at me, Jock," Jo cajoled, but there was no response. "Anybody home in there?" Jo joked uncertainly, her throat dry. Her sense of guilt grew as she watched Jock sit so deeply in thought that she had forgotten to be shy about her nudity. "Here," she said loudly, bundling Jock's housecoat and dumping it in her lap. "You'll catch your death of cold if you don't put this on."

"What?"

"Put your housecoat on, silly," Jo repeated with a nervous laugh.

"Oh." Jock wrapped her housecoat around her and lit another cigarette.

"Are you all right?" Jo asked.

Jock nodded and cleared her throat.

"Are you sure?"

Jock nodded again.

"What are you thinking about, then?"

The nod was replaced by a shrug and an expressive tilt of the head.

"Come on, Jock, talk to me," Jo said impatiently.

"I'm afraid you won't like me any more," Jock mumbled, her eyes on the far wall.

"Don't be silly."

"I'm not being silly."

"Oh yes you are."

"This changes everything," Jock replied hotly, turning to look at Jo.

Jo digested her flushed cheeks, her quivering lips, her brimming eyes and said, "Oh, Jock. We'll always be friends," even though she wasn't sure it was true. Where did they go from there? How could they retrace their steps now that the false intimacy artificially imposed by sharing a dorm room was no longer false? Could they revert to treating each other as roommates, sharing study space, their clothes and shoes and winter duds crammed into an inadequate closet, the two of them sleeping separately in single beds on opposite walls of the room? How would Jock feel when she went out with Blue, or if she found another lover? And for that matter, how would *she* feel? Could she withdraw from the intimacy, from the pleasure Jock had given her, from the force of Jock's love?

"Friends," Jock said, her voice neutral.

"Yes," Jo whispered as Jock turned to face her again.

"Friends," she said again, only this time it sounded like a curse.

Jo nodded. She felt like crying, because it was no good, no good at all. She would be a prisoner from this day forward, forced to think before she spoke, confined to half-truths and perhaps even outright lies to protect Jock from — but from what? She had never spoken of love, had never so much as hinted that anything more than friendship was involved. How had making love changed that? It must be possible to make love with a friend and still feel friendship.

"I think I'll go have a beer with Tony," Jock said, standing up and looping the belt of her housecoat tightly around her waist.

"Are you all right?" Jo asked.

Jock looked down at her, a complex smile transforming her features; for a moment her habitual look of innocence was replaced by a much older and wiser expression, but it was gone before Jo had a chance to react. "Sure. You?"

"Sure."

Suddenly Jock bent over and grasped Jo's shoulders, pulling her to her feet. Her kiss was intense, and Jo grew aroused immediately, matching her ferocity. Jock eventually pulled away, leaving Jo both wordless and astonished; what did it mean that one little kiss could make her pulse jump a notch, her breath come faster, her body yearn for more?

"Guess I'll go get that beer," Jock said casually, although her eyes were linked to Jo's, and the message in them was anything but casual.

Jo nodded, not trusting herself to speak.

"See you later."

Jo nodded again, and them flopped down on the bed, so confused that she hardly heard the door slam as Jock left.

# Dirty Words

Kate took one last look at herself in the mirror, staring at her sorry reflection. The make-up she had so carefully applied before leaving for work didn't hide the bruises or the swelling; probably nothing short of the inexorable passage of time would alter the visible proof of the beating she had received.

She felt so ashamed. How had her relationship with Maxine come to blows? What had she done wrong? Why had Maxine believed that she would tolerate that kind of treatment? She sighed and gently rubbed the thick sheet of make-up, attempting to make it smooth. There was no point in repeatedly asking herself the same questions, especially when they were the wrong ones. Down deep, she knew that it hadn't been her fault. She hadn't asked to be punched, and she hadn't asked to be raped. She had never, ever led Maxine to believe that sex without her permission would be acceptable. What Maxine had done was unfathomable, reprehensible, and entirely her own responsibility. Still, it was hard not to second-guess, and she couldn't help but wonder if she had somehow provoked Maxine. Perhaps she did share part of the blame. Perhaps if she had done things different-ly, it wouldn't have happened …

When she had pulled her abused body from bed Sunday morning, waking Jo in the process, she had wanted to be alone. She had longed for tranquillity, and to attain it, she needed solitude. Jo had been a godsend the night before, and Kate would always grateful for that. She would never have been able to cope if she had been alone during those first few hours. But come Sunday morning, she had no longer been capable of sharing her anguish. She had banished Jo without a glimmer of politeness, not even offering her coffee, much less break-fast. But that hadn't been important; she knew that Jo understood. No matter how closely Kate had clung to the younger woman all through the night, they didn't know each other. Smiles of recognition and the usual platitudes shouted in passing over the din of the bar didn't count for much once the immediacy of a crisis had passed and the process of healing started.

But the joys of solitude hadn't followed the dull thud of the door as a subdued, inarticulate Jo crept off. Kate had soaked in the bath, but it didn't make her feel any cleaner. She had wrapped herself in her favourite blanket, settled on the sofa and tried to read, but it hadn't worked. She hadn't been able to concentrate. And then the telephone had started to ring. The first time she made the mistake of picking it up, and of course it had been Maxine. She was mortified, she had said. She had a little too much of the old vino to drink, she had confessed. She had been so attracted to Kate that she couldn't control herself, she had averred. Not with all that vino inflaming her senses. She was oh so sorry, and she would never, ever do it again. Kate could trust her. Believe me, Maxine had insisted. And finally, I love you, I love you so much, I really do. I can't live without you. This said in a loud voice, with great urgency, as if loudness and urgency could turn the clock back and undo the deed.

Kate had felt sick to her stomach. How dare this woman talk to her about trust, with her cheek throbbing from blows inflicted by her fist and her vagina aching, chaffed raw by the rough penetration of her hand? Kate had listened, compelled by disbelief, but she hadn't replied. There was nothing to say. It was over. Nothing Maxine could do would repair the damage. She had finally dropped the telephone back into its cradle without uttering a word.

It had started to ring again, of course. Almost at once. Kate ignored it, although her pulse had quickened. Her answering machine had responded after the second ring. I know you're there, the voice had said. I know you're listening, it had continued. Kate bent forward and lowered the volume control, shutting out Maxine's voice. But she hadn't been able to shut out Maxine's presence, not completely, not when the telephone rang repeatedly, its shrill, cadenced persistence a silent but clear message that Maxine was not going to give up so easily. She had wiped her answering machine clean without listening to any of the messages. She knew that they would all be the same: I was a bad girl, but if you love me, you'll forgive me. I didn't mean to hurt you and I promise I'll never do it again. It was meaningless. It was nauseating. And it was a lie. She had heard enough. She hated the sound of Maxine's voice.

At two o'clock in the morning, after several hours of blessed silence, Maxine had begun to call again. Angry now, Kate picked up the telephone and told her to leave her alone. Period. Slam. Kate didn't know if this had worked or not, since she had immediately lowered the volume on both her telephone and her answering machine. But she still hadn't slept, and now she had dark circles under her eyes to add to the bruises on her cheek.

Well, staring at herself in the mirror in the women's washroom wasn't going to make it go away. Or get her work done. Kate gave herself a falsely valiant smile and went out to the ward.

"I fell," she announced before any of her fellow nurses had the opportunity to ask.

"Are you sure it wasn't a door knob?" quipped one of them with a nervous giggle.

"Or a fist?" said another with unaccustomed bluntness.

Everyone turned away, suddenly busy with chores which just seconds before they had all tacitly agreed could wait until they had finished the morning's first cup of coffee, over which the recent ward gossip would be aired. They were uncomfortable with the truth, Kate realized. And they felt threatened. After all, if it had happened to her, it could happen to any one of them. Being friends with a battered woman, even working with one, was dangerous. It brought the violence too close to home. She picked up a chart, any chart, thinking ruefully that after today, there would be no more speculation about the reason for her unmarried state or her sexual orientation. Everyone would assume that only a man could have done this to her.

"Ah, you're going in to see Ms. Dobbs?" asked the ward supervisor, studiously ignoring Kate's bruised cheek.

Kate looked down at the chart and realized that it was Oats'. "Well, I — "

"She certainly could use a good pep talk," the ward supervisor continued. "All she's doing is moping. Somebody has to talk some sense into her head or she'll be back in here in worse shape within the year. Or dead," she added bluntly.

The ward supervisor was right, of course, but how could Kate walk into Oats' room looking like this? She had thought to avoid Oats for a couple of days until the swelling had subsided and the bruises turned yellow and much easier to hide.

"Go on. You know her, after all. Perhaps she'll listen to you," the ward supervisor said, dismissing her with a commanding nod of her head.

Kate nodded back. She had her marching orders, and there was nothing else to be done. She opened the chart, frowning as she read. She could see that Oats was being her usual uncooperative self: refusing to get out of bed to exercise, not eating her meals and then demanding food at odd hours of the day or night, and even asking where the smoking room was. Kate grinned in spite of herself, and set off for Oats' room. Somebody had to talk some sense into that woman's head.

"Jesus Christ! What the hell happened to you?" Oats bellowed, startling her roommate, who was dozing in a chair while she waited for her husband. She was fully dressed, her handbag in her lap, her bulging suitcase sitting on the floor beside her chair.

"I fell," Kate lied. "I hear you've been doing your best to upset all the nurses," she swiftly continued in her sternest nurse's voice.

"Fell, hell! Somebody hit you," Oats said angrily, sitting up in bed, then easing her bare feet and legs out from under the covers.

Well, the one positive result of this fiasco with Maxine will be getting Oats out of bed, Kate thought, her mood swinging from amusement to despair. Why couldn't people just leave her alone?

"Who was it?" Oats asked, placing her feet on the floor and trying to stand up. "Oops!" she exclaimed, her mouth opening with surprise when her legs wobbled, threatening to collapse and dump her on the floor.

"Here — don't try to do everything all at once," Kate admonished, grasping Oats' arm to steady her. "Sit on the edge of the bed for awhile until the weakness passes."

"It must have been her husband, dearie," commented Oats' roommate. "It's always their husbands, you know."

Oats sat on the bed, looked at Kate for a long time and then said, "I don't believe it."

"It's true, dearie," added her roommate. "You think yours is different, but he never is."

"And I was the one who introduced you," Oats said miserably.

"Stole your man, did she? Well then, maybe she got what's coming to her," her roommate interjected.

This was impossible, Kate decided. Especially with Mrs. Neanderthal in the room with them. "Shall I get a wheelchair and take you for a ride?"

Oats nodded. "Sounds like a good idea."

"Watch out that she doesn't throw you down the steps, dearie," warned her roommate.

"Sure, sure."

Kate would have laughed except that her cheek hurt too much. With a polite smile at Mrs. Neanderthal, she left the room and went to the nurses' station, bringing a wheelchair back with her.

"Now remember what I told you," Oats' roommate said in a secretive voice.

"I will," Oats replied, letting Kate help her into the chair. "Wow! I never thought I'd feel like this!"

"Well, you haven't been on your feet for a long time. What did you expect?" Kate asked, wheeling her from the room.

"Don't start sounding like all those other biddies," Oats grumbled.

"It's my job," Kate reminded her.

"Correction: it's your job to be my friend," Oats said promptly, "and friends don't nag."

"Correction: friends should be the first ones to nag. If they don't, then they're not really friends," Kate replied just as swiftly.

"Where are you taking me?" Oats asked, adroitly changing the subject.

"To the sun room."

"Can I smoke there?"

"Oats, you can't smoke anywhere. If you do, it'll probably kill you," she said bluntly.

"I don't care," Oats blustered.

"Oh, but I think you do. And if you don't, you should," Kate retorted.

"Yeah, sure," Oats growled, momentarily defeated.

"And here we are," Kate announced with false cheerfulness, ignoring Oats' grumbling.

The sun room was deserted but not sunny; it was snowing again, big puffy flakes floating lazily through the air as if they were sentient and enjoying the free ride so much that they were in no hurry to arrive at their final destination.

"So Maxine beat you up," Oats said with surprising quietness as soon as Kate finished setting the brakes of the wheelchair and gingerly sitting down in a shabby armchair.

Kate nodded, tired of talking about it before she even started; it was going to be a long day.

"What else did she do to you?"

"Nothing," Kate replied, her eyes on her hands, which were folded neatly in her lap, professing a tranquillity she certainly didn't feel. If she raised them, tried to lift a cup of coffee or insert a thermometer or find a vein to give an injection, she was sure they would tremble and the coffee would slop out over the cup, the thermometer would snap, the needle miss its intended target. She hated that. She hated sloppiness, laxity, carelessness. She hated pushy people, women who were overbearing, who whined and begged and complained. Why then had she ever believed she was falling in love with Maxine, with her bad temper, her badgering, her jealousy, her possessiveness, her constant harping about Kate's reluctance to have sex?

"Kate. I saw how carefully you sat down. Now tell me the truth. What else did she do?" Oats persisted, leaning forward in the wheelchair, her expression intent.

"She raped me," Kate whispered. "And hit me when I fought back."

"Did you call the police?" Oats asked. "What did they say?"

"Oh, come on, Oats," Kate responded. "Call the police and say what? That my girlfriend raped me? They'd all get hard-ons. It would be better than a porn video. And besides, they'd never take it seriously. After all, how can a woman rape somebody? She hasn't got the right equipment," she added bitterly.

Oats frowned and settled back in the wheelchair. "Damn. I'm sorry, Kate. I knew Maxine had some rough edges, but I never imagined. I thought she would be okay when she found somebody and settled down. I'm really sorry."

"It's not your fault, Oats. She drinks too much, not that that's any excuse," Kate said.

"Just let me out of this place and I'll tell her a thing or two," Oats said vehemently.

"You just forget about Maxine, do you hear? It's over. She's out of my life forever," Kate said bitterly, lowering her face to hide the tears brimming in her eyes.

"What a mess," Oats said. "What a damn mess."

Kate closed her eyes and let the tears spill down her cheeks. She felt humiliated, and there was no safe place to hide. She didn't want Oats' sympathy, and she didn't want her plotting revenge, either. She just wanted to get through this one day at a time until she was capable of forgetting that it had ever happened. She fought to regain control and then said, "I hear Melba has been to see you."

"She came, we fought, I cried, she kissed me like there was no tomorrow, and then she left without saying another word," Oats synopsized glumly.

"Oh. Well, pardon me," Kate said, making an attempt at levity.

"Exactly. At least I think she did. Pardon me, I mean," Oats added.

"That's a step in the right direction," Kate commented, wiping the last of the tears from her eyes with the back of her hand.

"Yeah, but which direction? You know, I don't really understand that woman," Oats confessed. "I don't know what she wants."

"Maybe she doesn't know either," Kate suggested.

"Melba? Hell, she knows everything," Oats said with a dry chuckle.

"Don't be so sure about that."

"Why not? She is," Oats retorted.

Kate smiled even though it hurt her cheek; Oats was miffed because Melba had succeeded in breaking down her defences. What else was new?

"And stop taking Melba's side," Oats scolded.

"Me? I'm not taking anybody's side in anything," Kate replied. "I've got enough problems of my own to worry about, in case you haven't noticed."

Oats rolled her eyes and managed to look guilty at the same time. "I haven't forgotten. I'll never forget. It's just a matter of time and opportunity, but Maxine is dead meat."

"Oats," Kate said warningly.

"As soon as I win the lottery, I'll put a contract out on her," Oats continued, oblivious to Kate's stern face.

"Oats!"

"Or I'll hire a mercenary, a hit man, and tell him to take it slow, one limb at a time," Oats went on.

"Oh, shut up," Kate snapped, stifling a laugh. Whatever the heart attack had damaged, it sure hadn't been Oats' mouth.

"That's better," Oats said calmly, a self-satisfied look on her face.

"Bitch."

"All these compliments will give me a thick head."

"Better than a fat bum."

"I've got one of those, too."

Kate started to laugh and at first it felt good, releasing tension, cleansing some of the poison from her mind. But then she couldn't stop; tears poured from her eyes and splashed on her uniform, and suddenly she was crying, sobbing uncontrollably.

"Ah, Kate."

"Never mind," she snuffled, shaking her head. "Just never mind."

"But I do mind, Kate, I really do," Oats replied earnestly.

"I know," Kate sighed. "I love you too."

"Ah yes, love," Oats said musingly.

"Today's dirty word," Kate said, laughing through her tears.

"Yesterday's, today's, tomorrow's — who's being choosy? I mean, love makes the world go round, and all that stupid nonsense. Well, somebody has sold the world a bill of worthless goods," Oats expounded bitterly.

"It's not as bad as all that," Kate protested, licking salty tears from her lips.

"No, it's worse. Fall in love and lose your life," Oats continued harshly. "Look at you, for god's sake. All you wanted was a little loving, something to make the days go by and the nights more interesting, and look what you ended up with. Being knocked around and — and — hurt."

"That wasn't love," Kate said quietly. Nobody would ever convince her that Maxine had been motivated by love. Greed, anger, self-loathing, hatred of women, even stupidity, but not love. Never love. Love had nothing to do with violence, with what Maxine had done to her.

But Oats continued as if she hadn't heard Kate. "And then take a look at me, will you? I'm nearly fifty, and I can't even love another woman."

"That's not true," Kate protested.

"Oh, sure. I've been in love a million times, but you of all people know exactly what that means. Sex, sex, and then more sex. And after that, sex, sex, and more sex with another woman. And so on down the line."

"I thought it was different with Melba."

"So did I," Oats said glumly. "Believe me, so did I."

"I thought you were really in love with her," Kate persisted.

"Yeah, I was. And look where it got me," Oats said, gesturing around the visiting room.

"What on earth are you talking about?"

"I fell in love with Melba and ended up with a broken heart," Oats stated dramatically.

Kate burst out laughing.

"Hey! It's not funny!"

Kate clamped her mouth shut to stop her laughter. "I'm sure it's not, but you know, Oats, you got what you deserved. You can't cheat on a woman like Melba and expect her to sit quietly on the sidelines and watch you make a fool of her."

Oats frowned like she had smelled something bad, and then a look of tired disgust appeared on her face. "You're right, of course. You're absolutely right. But Melba is so rigid. She won't listen to anything which doesn't fit into her narrow little scheme of things. She has all these rules, and everything has to happen just so, in a certain way and in a certain order."

"And order drives you crazy," Kate added.

"You're darn right," Oats replied. "It's like growing up in my mother's house all over again. Take your shoes off, don't slam the back door, don't sit on that sofa with your dirty clothes on, wash your face, your hands, your ears, your neck, your unmentionables before you dare sit down at the dinner table, don't wear that to school, what do you mean, you haven't got a date. Or having to sit still in school for hours on end. Do this now, that then. Melba's rules are emotional, but it's the same thing. Don't tell me you love me, it's too soon for you to know. Well, how can she be sure? Who gave her the right to put love on a schedule, to put *me* on a schedule? And what kind of thing is that to say to a woman in the throes of passion? Talk about the death — no, the premeditated murder — of romance!"

Kate shrugged, amused. Oats had obviously met her match, but she wasn't going to be the one to tell her. Let her figure it out for herself.

"It's enough to drive me around the bend," Oats muttered.

"So why don't you tell her how you feel?" Kate suggested.

"I have, believe me, I have. But she just stops for a minute, looks at me in that funny way of hers and then continues on as if I hadn't said a word," Oats said.

"Well, you can't turn to me for solutions; I've managed to make such a mess of my life that I couldn't possibly offer any sensible advice," Kate said with a glance at her watch. "Look at that — we've been sitting here talking for almost half an hour. I've got to get back to work!"

"Have you any idea when I'm going to be released?" Oats asked as Kate rose stiffly from the chair.

"No, but I'll see if I can find out," Kate replied. "Do you want me to take you back to your room?"

"No. I think I'll stay here for awhile and enjoy the scenery," Oats replied.

"Don't overdo it," Kate warned her, walking over and smoothing the blanket covering Oats' lap and legs.

"There's no danger of that," Oats replied glumly, looking around the deserted sun room. "What, do you think I'm going to have a wild party in here all by myself?"

"Want some magazines?" Kate asked.

"Naw. I'm tired of reading chicken soup recipes or how to cook a meal for forty-five in ten minutes or how to keep your husband interested," Oats said.

"I'm sorry our reading material isn't up to your standards," Kate replied with a laugh.

"Never mind. I'll just sit here like a sedate old lady and watch the snow come down," Oats said with an edge of martyrdom in her voice.

"Fine. Whatever turns you on," Kate answered. "Anyway, I've got to go. I'll come back later to see how you're doing."

"Maybe I'll have lunch here and give my charming roommate time to clear out," Oats suggested.

"Well, we'll see how you feel in an hour or so."

"Yeah."

Kate gave Oats a soft kiss on the top of the head and left her alone in the sun room. She was behind in her morning schedule, and as she walked down the corridor, she mentally listed the temps and blood pressures which had to be taken, the pills and injections which had to be given, the patients she had to prep for tests later in the day or for operations early tomorrow morning. And the whispered questions from worried men and women who needed reassurance, questions which were more often than not difficult or downright impossible to answer. She was tempted to disappear into the women's room for a second, to reassure herself that her inexpert make-up job was holding up and that her bruises were no more visible than when she had first walked into the hospital this morning, but time was pressing. She was so far behind in her schedule that she would probably have to skip lunch, which was not all that unusual.

Life goes on, she told herself, rounding a corner and pushing open the door to a room, concerned at the sight of a post-op patient who was obviously in pain. "Having some pain, Madame Duval?" she asked in French. "It's time for your next injection," she added after consulting her chart and glancing at her watch. "I'll be right back."

Life goes on, she thought again, walking swiftly to the nurses' station. Unless you're dead. As long as you're alive, whether through stubborn perseverance or just plain dumb luck, you might as well accept it.

# The Wrong Menu

"**I** guess I'd better go," Jock said, wondering if Candy was awake. She studied the freckled back of the comatose woman sprawled beside her in the dishevelled bed, sighed, and lit a cigarette. Three nights with the same woman and she was already eager to be done with it, to move on to different if not greener pastures. But it wasn't Candy's fault, she decided. No, the problem was her. Her cowardice, not to mention her inability to accept the truth. Yes, when the going gets tough, the weak, mealy mouthed and generally incapable get going. Jock sighed again and lay back on the pillow, puffing on her cigarette and grimacing as a barely recognizable smoke ring floated toward the paint-blistered ceiling. If she smoked until she was a hundred, she would still never get it right.

"Candy? Are you awake?" she ventured. Candy snored in response and turned over, one hand coming to rest on Jock's bare belly. She blew another wretched smoke ring in the general direction of the ceiling and then gave up. It was too frustrating. She knew she would be able to blow the perfect smoke ring if she didn't have so much on her mind. And she wouldn't have so much on her mind if she could just get a grip on her love life. How had she suddenly managed to go from being a virgin with a batting average of zero to having two lovers? And why had she taken up residence in Candy's sordid bed for three days and three nights when what she had wanted more than anything in the world for longer than she could remember was to be Jo's lover?

"Damn it, are you going to sleep all day?" she complained, putting out her cigarette and staring agitatedly at Candy, willing her to wake up. After all those years of being part of the in-crowd in high school, of being first string in every sport she ever played, of being better than most at nearly everything, she had ended up in the bed of the wrong woman. A neurotic, pool-playing university drop-out who was never the same twice. A punk who claimed that she was a woman of the world but who drank too much, never changed her sheets or dusted her Sally Ann furniture, rarely seemed to wash and never used deodorant even though she had strong body odour which was compelling only when Jock was horny. She felt cheated; her fantasies about love and sex had been riddled with holes before she had had a chance to enjoy them. Where was the romance? Oh sure, she had been attracted to Candy, but after what had happened with Jo, she probably would have been satisfied with any cockroach of a woman. And sure, she had been enthusiastic, even after Candy had got drunk as a skunk on cheap corner-store wine that first night and had fallen asleep in the middle of making love. Certain things can be overlooked when you really need somebody, and Jock had been so desperate that she would have forgiven anybody almost anything. So she had permitted Candy to soothe her wounded spirit after Jo had let her down so badly with that ill-timed proclamation of continued friendship. Some friendship, she snorted scornfully. Jo had been turned on too, so what gave her the right to think that Jock would be fool enough to believe that their attraction to each other meant nothing, that making love was just a one-time exception in an otherwise sexless relationship? How could Jo pretend that nothing had happened and insist that they could easily revert to just being pals?

"God, I'm hung over! What time is it?" Candy mumbled, opening her eyes. They were bloodshot.

"Late."

"Get me an orange juice and a couple of painkillers, will you?"

Jock got out of bed, padded into the kitchen, and rinsed out two dirty glasses. She poured an orange juice for Candy and a glass of water for herself; the orange juice was sour, slightly off, but Candy didn't seem to care.

"The painkillers," Candy said dully as Jock handed her the glass.

"Coming up," Jock replied, putting her glass of water on the stained bedside table and returning to the kitchen. The large bottle of pharmacy brand painkillers was sitting on the counter beside the dish detergent. Pills seemed to play an integral part in Candy's diet, and having witnessed Candy's heavy drinking, Jock could understand why.

"Here." Jock handed Candy two pills, which she swiftly chewed and swallowed, using the orange juice as a chaser.

"Give me a few minutes and I'll be just fine," Candy told her.

"I'll take a shower, then," Jock said.

"Not into it this morning?" Candy replied, lowering the dingy sheet to her waist.

"I think I'd better get back to the dorm and do some studying," Jock answered, turning away. The room smelled bad; there was too much of Candy's body odour in the air, and there had been too many days and nights of unwashed sex. Even her own smell turned her off.

"You could study me instead," Candy said suggestively, kicking the sheet completely off.

Jock laughed uncomfortably and shrugged.

"Oh, well," Candy said lightly, noting Jock's disinterest. "Go take your shower."

Relieved, Jock left the bedroom. The bathroom was so dirty that she left the light off so she wouldn't have to look at the grime coating the sink and the dark rim of soap scum circling the bathtub. She turned on the shower and regulated the water, then stepped into the tub. There was barely enough spray to activate the shower or to keep her warm in the unheated room, but she took her time washing her hair with Candy's shampoo, thoroughly scrubbed her body with a sliver of soap, and then stood patiently under the trickle of water to rinse off. At least she would feel clean in body, but her mind was another matter. Why had she run away from Jo? Hadn't that last kiss at least partially turned the tables on Jo's protestation that they were just friends? There had to be a way to make Jo listen, not just to what Jock had to say but to her own feelings, and if anyone was capable of finding it, Jock should be.

After all, they had been friends since they were in diapers; they knew each other better than anybody else. They had never really talked about being gay, but somehow they had both known about the other without ever needing to say anything. Jo had been the only person Jock had ever admired, and typically, she never did anything halfway. She had always been a little bit in love with Jo, and the forced proximity of sharing a room with her, all those glimpses of Jo's body as she dressed and undressed, the scent of her cologne, the cute little snores which made Jock smile in the night, even the familiar smell of her dirty laundry had worked their magic on Jock: she was well and truly infatuated. Before they had made love, she had accepted the fact that Jo didn't feel the same way. She had known that Jo had never been attracted to her, but it hadn't mattered; love wasn't something you could turn on and off like a light switch. But now it was different; she had tasted the real thing, and her body longed for the touch of Jo's eyes, the stroke of her hands, the soft wetness of her mouth. It made her sick to her stomach when she thought about Jo in bed with Blue. Or with any other woman but herself, for that matter.

And now she knew what sex was like: the fierce hunger of one woman for another, the hot weakness, the sweet wetness, the close, trembling intensity, the feelings of love, of power and submission. Her ability to give Jo such pleasure had been tantamount to a miracle. Where had that untapped, wonderful knowledge come from? Had she been born with it?

She stepped out the shower and shivered. Nothing would ever be the same again. *She* would never be the same again. Knowing what she knew now about sex, about women and especially about Jo, how could she avoid putting this new knowledge to use? There would be new meanings to read into each little gesture, every innocent word would have to be reinterpreted, even the most insignificant touch re-evaluated, not to mention nuances heard, seen and felt. Her frame of reference had suddenly exploded, expanded to infinity. She felt both humble and afraid, because she found it difficult to imagine staring infinity in the face. What was she supposed to see? How was she expected to respond?

"Jock? Are you still in there?"

"Yes," she replied, wrapping the towel around her and reluctantly opening the door.

"I think I'm going to be sick."

Oh no.

Candy rushed in, still naked, and went down on her knees before the toilet.

"Oh."

I am not, I repeat *not*, going to hold her head, Jock thought resolutely as Candy started to retch. "Here," she said, pushing a wad of toilet paper into Candy's hand.

Her thanks was another retch. Anyway, it's her own fault for drinking too much, Jock decided, feeling both disgust and guilt as she stood looking down at her lover.

"Water," Candy croaked.

Jock combatted rising nausea at the smell and gave Candy a glass of water.

"More pills."

Jo would never get drunk like this, she thought despairingly as she made her way back to the kitchen and shook another two pills from the bottle.

"Here."

"Thanks."

Nothing was working out right. Where was the ecstasy, the happiness? Candy made her feel jaded, tired, depressed. But she was with the wrong woman, and that wasn't Candy's fault. Thinking about Jo made her feel sad, because she had likely lost her best friend, not to mention the only woman she had ever really loved. Perhaps it would have been better to pine over an impossibility than to deal with this mess. Her dreams had come true, but what difference did that make if they didn't *stay* true?

"I've got to go," Jock said desperately.

"Yeah. I know," Candy said, standing up, wiping her face with the wad of toilet paper Jock had given her.

"Really," Jock repeated.

"I understand," Candy said with a sigh. "Anyway, this isn't your scene, is it?"

Jock opened her mouth and closed it again.

"You don't have to say anything," Candy said, smiling cynically, suddenly looking like the quintessential bar dyke.

"But — "

"Three days is long enough, I think," Candy interrupted. "You're starting to bore me."

Jock was speechless.

"Oh, you're nice, but you're young, and you need to develop your imagination," Candy continued.

What the hell was she talking about?

"Increase your repertoire," Candy explained. "You know."

No she didn't, but Jock wasn't going to admit it. "You should talk," she sputtered.

Candy laughed. "Oh, sure, I drink too much. Don't think I didn't notice you looking down your nose at me."

"Well, I though it would have been better without all that booze," Jock said defensively.

"How the hell would you know?" Candy snapped, pushing by Jock. "And don't tell me you don't ever get drunk," she added over her shoulder.

Jock flushed the toilet, drank a glass of water and had the good sense to realize that this was way beyond her. She didn't understand Candy at all, and the sooner she got out of there, the better.

"I need my clothes," she said, knocking on the bedroom door.

"Well, come on in and get them," Candy replied.

Jock slowly opened the door and looked in. Candy was standing in front of a cracked mirror hanging crookedly on the wall, calmly combing her hair into place. She was already dressed in black jeans and a black tank top.

"Don't mind me," she said, turning to Jock. "Sometimes I get a little testy, especially when I feel really hung over."

"Sure," Jock replied guardedly.

"You're not so bad," Candy continued, turning back to the mirror and giving her hair one last upward twist. "You're just young. But you'll grow out of it."

Thanks a million, Jock thought sourly. Just as long as I don't grow into someone like you. She plucked her stale clothes from the back of a chair and dressed.

"Give me a call when you've got a minute," Candy said abruptly.

"Sure," Jock replied, although she was already quite positive that she would never have another minute to spare for the rest of her life.

"We can still have some fun once in awhile," Candy added, following Jock from the bedroom.

"Whatever," Jock responded politely, trying not to look like she was overly eager to escape.

"It's been nice," Candy said.

"Yeah," Jock averred with an insincere smile. She closed the door behind her with an inner sigh of relief and bounded down three flights of stairs to the front door. Did Candy mean nice as in enjoyable or nice as in boring? Jock would never know. And get a repertoire, she had said. Well, if only it was that easy. If only you could slip into a sex shop and choose the repertoire you wanted from a menu, just like you could in your neighbourhood restaurant. Two big fried eggs, over easy, three slabs of bacon dripping with grease, wholewheat toast slathered with butter and a steaming cup of strong coffee. Come to think of it, when had she last had something to eat? She slid her hand into her pocket, pulled out two five dollar bills and decided that breakfast was in order, even though it was late in the day. Whether her repertoire was adequate or not, she was positive that life was always better on a full stomach.

# Crossroads

$\mathbf{M}$elba turned off her computer, locked her office and retrieved her coat from the closet. She waited for the elevator, smiling at several familiar faces as the door slid open. It was nearly six o'clock, but the elevator was crowded; hardly anyone working in the office tower left on time at four-thirty, and she was no exception, even when her mind was anywhere but on her work. Like now.

When she had been very young, in her early twenties, becoming a financial consultant had seemed like the pinnacle of success. Getting there had taken single-minded perseverance, long, weary nights of concentrated study and years of apprenticeship in small and then medium-sized companies. Still, she had never wanted to be anything else, and when she had triumphed over hundreds of other qualified candidates for this particular job, she had been hard pressed to keep from walking around her new office with a euphoric smile on her face.

It was different now. After nearly twenty years her skills were well-developed and the work seemed easy, and although promotions came swiftly at first, she had eventually crashed headlong into the inevitable glass ceiling which had stopped her from progressing further up the ladder. Corporate wisdom dictated that women should be relegated to support positions (read secretarial and clerical), and the only concession her company made to the pressure of the women's movement and government equity regulations was to grudgingly admit that a few persons of the female sex might be suitable for middle management posts. Women certainly weren't invited to share the breathtaking view from the top, to inhabit those large, corner offices with their prestigious floor-to-ceiling windows and their sleek, relentlessly hetero private secretaries who dressed like Greta Garbo, could make up their faces in ten seconds flat, typed a million words a minute without damaging so much as an edge of the thick lacquer covering their fingernails, took shorthand in their sleep, smiled when they made coffee, and never spoke above an efficient, civilized murmur. Indeed, tough, take-charge women willing to perpetually stand behind their bosses were so scarce that more effort was made to secure their services than to pull in a big client or, in fact, to prepare women for management positions. And to her undying resentment, some of the best were paid almost as much as Melba.

After her painful encounter with the glass ceiling, it hadn't taken Melba long to lose the commendable (if innocent) belief that the sky was the limit. If there was no conceivable way to get to the top, why should she work her butt off trying? So she settled into a rather mindless routine, her work competent but unexciting, her exuberance tamed. The end result was boredom and increasing dissatisfaction, especially when she thought of the totally predictable progression of years stretching to retirement. It seemed like infinity, and infinite monotony was enervating.

Perhaps that was why she turned to women who were unpredictable. Like Sue, who she refused to call Oats, as if that refusal would somehow change her, make the worst excesses of her quixotic nature disappear and force her to develop her better qualities. Not surprisingly, it didn't work; Sue could be soft, loving and dependable one minute, rough, unpredictable and selfish the next.

Sue had been the latest in a series of women who were — in a word — wild. Women who could be outlandish, uninhibited and often vulgar, and who were more often than not gluttonous about food, alcohol, drugs, sex, life. Who were not fond of safety and therefore set no limits. Or very few, just enough to stay alive. Who took you with them on their undisciplined and sometimes dangerous escapades. Melba went willingly, intent on escaping the humdrum world of high finance, the tedium of number-crunching, the mindless business of convincing clients that it was good judgement to buy on the way down, then placating them when the market fell even further before turning around. It was modern-day, Bay Street alchemy: smoke without fire, bulk without substance, illusion without reality. Except that this particular illusion was real; people got richer when she made the right decisions at the right time and invested their money at the opportune moment, relying on her judgement and nerves of steel to hold off selling until the last possible second. None of it meant a damn, of course; she wasn't contributing anything useful to the world. No, all she was doing was helping them pad their pocketbooks, making the rich even richer. And since it was easier to dislike her clients rather than herself, she grew to despise them. Most of them were already obscenely rich, and yet not one possessed the good sense to know when to stop and enjoy it. They hoarded their money and spent it only when they absolutely had to. But who knows — maybe she too would love money for its own sake; she had never had enough of the stuff to find out.

Melba's lovers squandered what they had and then more. They had no faith in what tomorrow would bring, so they spent their todays in endless pursuit of immediate gratification. Their tastes were unrefined but vast; they displayed the same enthusiasm for a lavishly prepared, gourmet meal in one of the best French restaurants as they did for junk food served on a cracked plate in a greasy spoon, upended a jug of convenience store rotgut with the same gusto as a bottle of fine wine, waxed poetic over a weekend spent at an exclusive ski resort in the Laurentiens and yet thought that huddling under a leaking tent in a chilly, mosquito-ridden field was the epitome of romance. It didn't take much to make them happy, but they had to be busy and always on the move to something or someone new. Otherwise boredom set in as swiftly as mildew in a damp basement.

Until she met Sue Dobbs, Melba had never tried to reform one of her "wild" women. Through experience, she had learned to leave well enough alone, to enjoy them for what they were, to appreciate the lack of restraint they brought into her life. At their urging she sometimes experienced the verboten, doing things her conservative nature would otherwise never have permitted her to do. She danced the night away in dank and undoubtedly dangerous waterfront clubs, ate too much greasy food in ill-lit, all-night cafes, frittered away her money on drinks with fancy names, meals in overpriced restaurants and weekend escapes in hotels with adult videos, mirrors on the ceiling and beds which vibrated, gambled with fate in fast cars driven by inebriated women, got drunk on smooth Bordeaux and on gassy beer, spent long hours in conversation with persons of ambiguous sex, frequented bars with crass strip shows and artless performances by untalented transvestites sporting unnaturally coloured wigs, elaborate gowns, shaved legs and five-inch spike heels. Actually, they weren't all that different from some of the corporate secretaries populating her office, but this little secret remained very much her own, providing her with a way of retaining her sense of humour when these latter-day Garbos looked down their noses at her, as they unvaryingly did.

Encouraged by lovers who populated the fringes of lesbian life, women who had seen the void and scornfully laughed into it, Melba experimented with sex. It always took place at arm's length, as if her real self was hovering over her shoulder, protecting her from harm, from being appalled by what she was doing, from feeling shocked, humiliated, and sometimes, disgusted. But in the end, she had to admit that it was all as boring as her job. How many drunk women say anything interesting? And how did an anorexic, coiffed, stoned transvestite crooning Barry Manilow into a microphone — which he from time to time pretended to take into his open, lipsticked mouth, much to the lewd amusement of the crowd — add to the quality of her life? There was no doubt she was bemused by the chubby, middle-aged butch with Elvis hair, who, dressed in a black suit which was so tight that her bulges were clearly visible, performed torrid torch songs and made the young, longhaired femmes squeal when she shook her head and heavy beads of sweat dropped from her to them in a sort of ritual baptism. Where did a woman like that come from? Was she living as a man? Could anybody be that butch and still feel like a woman? Melba didn't know, and there was no one to ask. She looked like — and felt like — a tourist passing through, so it wasn't surprising that they wouldn't confide in her. At least the people inhabiting this netherworld seemed to be capable of communicating with one another, which was fortunate for them.

She had sex with women she didn't know, and it meant nothing to her, never touching her personally, never threatening her integrity. Her interest was piqued by the unknown, by the prospect of sex with strangers, with her lover participating as passionate voyeur, or by experimenting with sex toys brazenly purchased in a drab sex shop where everything was covered with plastic, more to keep it clean than to hide it from view. But all of it left her feeling titillated rather than satisfied, as if she herself had been the voyeur, squinting through a peephole for her ten dollars worth of fake sex, or masturbating to the incredibly bad acting in a lesbian porn video purchased in San Francisco or Provincetown and smuggled over the border.

Never mind, she thought, using her remote control to deactivate the car alarm, then opening the door. Sue had been different, although perhaps she had been foolish to believe that. There was no denying that Sue had been wild, fully living her Oats' incarnation. But right from the beginning, from the moment Melba had asked her to dance that fateful evening last fall in l'Entr'acte, she had sensed that there was something more. Sue had seemed to have the potential to grow, to change, to care deeply, and Melba had been certain that under that brusque exterior, there was a sensitive nature waiting to be nurtured. Sue had wanted to love somebody, but she just hadn't known how.

Well, fool that she was, Melba had thought that she could show her. Unfortunately, in the showing, she had fallen in love. Look, miracles do happen. It had worked, for awhile, anyway, until Sue had betrayed her with Frédérique. In her futile and essentially meaningless dalliances over the years, Melba had become accustomed to suspending value judgements, temporarily compromising her moral standards and generally overlooking a certain amount of ambiguity. But some things were not negotiable, and laxity with the truth was the most important of these. Sue had professed love, agreed to monogamy and then the minute Melba's attention had been elsewhere for a brief instant, she had cruised Frédérique, thoughtlessly taking her home and making love with her in the bed she and Melba shared. In this instance, the truth was so archetypical that it was almost trite: nothing mattered when a butch was on the prowl. She would probably have betrayed her own mother when her hormones were raging. Or her best friend. And her lover. Yes, most certainly her lover.

Melba drove into the garage, reset the car alarm and then locked the car. She hated high rises; it was bad enough to work in one, but here she was living in a fourteenth floor, nondescript, beige apartment with low ceilings. At least the rooms were large, and she had negotiated a good deal on a sublet. She had not had any other choice. She couldn't have stayed with Sue, not after Frédérique. She rode the elevator to the fourteenth floor, remembering how shocked she had been, standing just inside the bedroom door with that stupid, nearly illiterate love note crushed in her hand, looking down on Sue's plump nakedness. A totally unfamiliar jealousy had inflamed her, clouding her emotions. Sue was incorrigible; she would never change. So Melba had cut her losses and run. It had been the only logical thing to do. She had escaped back into her own world, where the rules were prescribed, the demarcations clear, the boundaries impossible to transgress. And where there were no unpleasant surprises. She had gone home, emotionally, spiritually, intellectually.

This was not cowardice, she told herself firmly as she unlocked the flimsy, hollow-core door to her apartment and switched on the overhead living-room light. It took courage to leave someone you loved instead of staying until love turned to hatred, bitterness to despairing acceptance, desire to a shrunken, mocking image of itself. That this turn of events was not inevitable was something she didn't stop to consider. After all, she had years of experience with women like Sue, and in the end, each and every relationship had turned sour. Many of them had been unreliable, forgetting about dates, leaving her stranded in restaurants, bars, bus terminals and even airports. Most of them cheated, even though they had promised to be faithful. Sometimes they had cruised other women right in front of her, which had both embarrassed and angered her. Some were too crude for words once she really got to know them, while others asked for sexual favours Melba found impossible to grant. From time to time one of them fell deeply in love with her, forcing her to extricate herself from a relationship which threatened to smother her. She couldn't abide the possessiveness of a butch unused to being in love; the obsessive questioning, the jealous reaction to every perceived threat, the attempt to isolate her from friends and acquaintances, the domination, the expectation of unquestioned loyalty and obedience.

Melba dropped her suit jacket on a chair, kicked off her high heels and flopped down on the sofa. Why couldn't Sue have been different? Yeah, sure, if she was going to dream about the impossible, why not hope to be president of her company? She might as well believe in the tooth fairy, or the man in the moon, or the Loch Ness monster. Although there was some talk about that being real ...

Give it up, she told herself, punching the play button on her answering machine.

"Melba? It's Kate. Give me a call when you get home, okay? Bye." Melba frowned and pressed the pause button. Kate probably wanted to talk about Sue, but she was sick and tired of thinking about Sue every waking minute of the day and night. And she was also sick and tired of feeling guilty. But there was no way around it; she would have to call Kate back.

She sighed and released the pause button.

"Hello Melba. It's Maxine, Kate's friend. I wonder if you could give me a call."

That was strange, Melba thought as she wrote down Maxine's telephone number. What did Maxine want? She was an old friend of Sue's, and now Kate's lover, or so Melba assumed. Was she going to be yet another bearer of platitudes, promoting the turning of cheeks, so long as it wasn't one of her own, shamelessly quoting the old saw that to forgive is divine, especially now that Sue had been felled by a heart attack? If yet another sanctimonious fool added her voice to that insidious, guilt-provoking chorus, she would be tempted to smite her on the spot. Melba wasn't the cheek-turning type, and it wasn't her fault that Sue had had a heart attack. She had to call Kate, but Maxine? Forget it. She would call back if it was important.

She picked up the phone and dialled Kate's number.

"Hello."

"Kate? It's Melba."

"Oh hi, Melba. I'm glad you called."

I bet you are, Melba thought murderously, wishing she had stopped to mix a martini before tackling Kate.

"Anyway, I was wondering if you had thought about Oats," Kate continued uncomfortably.

"What do you mean? Of course I have — didn't she tell you I went to visit her?" Melba replied impatiently. Sue had cried. And acted like she loved her. And then Melba had kissed her. Whatever had possessed her? Anger? Love? Revenge? A little of each?

"No, I mean, Oats is going to be released soon, and I just wondered if you had thought about that," Kate continued uncertainly.

Melba could see it all coming now. "You aren't really suggesting that I take her in, are you? Because if you are, think again!" Suddenly the telephone receiver was back in its stand, the cord dangling over the arm of the sofa. The violence of her reaction shook her. Had she really hung up on Kate?

Chagrined, she picked up the receiver and dialled again. "Sorry."

"That's okay. I didn't mean to imply anything — I just thought that you should know."

"When is she going to be released?"

"In the next couple of days. They just want to be sure her medication is working," Kate replied.

"I see. Well, thanks for telling me," Melba said, fiddling with an earring.

"Look, she can come and stay with me, I've got plenty of room, but I just thought that — "

"Let me think about it, will you?" Melba interrupted wearily.

"Sure."

"And do me a favour, will you?"

"What?"

"Call off the dogs," Melba said bluntly.

"What on earth are you talking about?"

"I just had a message from Maxine on my machine," Melba replied.

"Maxine?"

"You know, Maxine. Your girlfriend."

"Oh no."

"Well, you can tell her I won't be calling her back," Melba added.

"No, please don't," Kate said quietly. "I mean, don't call her."

"You know, I don't appreciate all the pressure you've been putting on me," Melba said. "Sue really hurt me, and yet you expect me to forget all about it. Well, I'm sorry, but I can't turn my feelings on and off like a tap, not like some people I know."

"But I didn't ask Maxine to call you," Kate explained. "And please, please don't call her. We're not seeing each other any more."

"Oh." Melba was nonplussed; if Kate hadn't asked Maxine to contact her, then why did she call? "Maybe I should. Maybe she was calling about something else."

"Don't."

Melba's eyes widened at the sound of Kate's voice. "Why on earth not? It could be important."

"She probably wants to tell you her side of the story," Kate said, her tone bitter.

Melba laughed. "My dear, I've heard one too many stories from the Maxine's of this world to have the wool pulled over my eyes. But she is a friend of Sue's. Perhaps Sue asked her to call me."

"I doubt it," Kate replied.

Melba waited for Kate to continue, but when no explanation was forthcoming, her curiosity was piqued. "Let me know if I'm prying, but what — "

"Look, you may as well know. Oats will probably tell you anyway. Maxine forced herself on me."

Melba was speechless. Some women liked to play rough, but she had avoided their games, refusing to enter their playrooms, or "torture chambers," as she had laughingly called them when describing to Sue one rather persistent admirer's tactics to win her approval to a night — just one — of bondage. Just to try it on for size. But Melba had known that it would never fit, and the thought of experimenting with something so alien had left her cold. But hard to imagine as it was, Maxine obviously hadn't been playing games or simply acting out one of her fantasies. Had she gone crazy? "But — I thought you were lovers." Not that it mattered, she realized immediately; lovers could and did rape.

"So did everyone. But we weren't," Kate responded.

"Well. I don't know what to say," Melba admitted.

"There really isn't anything you can say," Kate said with an audible sigh. "Just don't call her. She's dangerous."

"I'll say," Melba remarked. Who would have guessed that Maxine was capable of violence? Melba had been introduced to most of Sue's friends. She had liked some, disliked most and tolerated others, but Maxine had left her indifferent. She found her insipid, always trying to act like a big shot, telling jokes which were tasteless and unamusing. She rarely had a original thought of her own, and she following Sue around from bar to bar and escapade to escapade like a puppy dog certain of being rewarded with a bone if it behaved well.

"Look, are you busy tonight?" Kate asked abruptly.

"Ah, no, not really," Melba replied, ruefully thinking of the low-cal microwave dinner waiting in her freezer and the unfinished book sitting beside the remote control to her television. "Want to come over?" she asked with forced enthusiasm.

"Why don't you come here instead? I've got a pot of chili sitting in the fridge," Kate responded.

"I'm a vegetarian."

"It's meatless."

It was useless to protest. Her microwave dinner would have to wait. "Sure. Want me to bring dessert?"

"Great!"

"At seven?"

"Why not right now? I'll set the table and put the pot on the stove."

"Okay."

"See you soon."

"Right."

Should she change? Get out of her skirt, panty hose, high heels? Switch from what she jokingly called her work uniform into her dyke one? She hadn't the energy, and besides, she didn't think Kate would notice whether she showed up wearing a ball gown or her paint-stained jeans. And if she did notice, she wouldn't care. Kate wanted company, somebody to ward off Maxine's lingering ghost. And since Sue was in the hospital, she was elected for tonight. Well, it was the least she could do for a friend, she thought, stuffing her feet back into her heels, pausing for a moment to register surprise that she considered Kate to be a friend. She picked up her jacket, smiling at herself; why was she always amazed when she made a new friend? Or discovered that she still desperately wanted to be with a lover she had just discarded?

If she wasn't careful, she thought with a wry chuckle, she was going to damage her self-image as a businesswoman who dabbled in the emotions, much like a weekend artist fiddling with oils on canvas. But then, some self-images were vintage, deserving of careful nurturance and preservation, while others were simply utilitarian, to be disposed of as soon as they outlived their usefulness. But imagine not knowing which was which at her age. When she had been an innocent girl of sixteen, she couldn't wait to grow up, because adults were free to do anything. From the hindsight of fifty, she realized that the real challenge was to overcome the paralysis of self-doubt and to establish a workable identity. When it came to the final analysis, who you were was not at all who you might prefer to be, and the struggle for self-respect, self-knowledge and contentment was a lifelong one.

It was ironic, she thought, locking the door behind her, that she was successful in her career, earned a high salary and made millions for her clients, and yet she hadn't found a lover who could make her happy. Oh, she could probably have a long line of potential suitors standing on her door step with a simple snap of her fingers, but her aim was off and she always chose badly. And the reason for that was the one question she was still incapable of answering.

# Double Trouble

J o woke up grumbling and leapt out of bed, grimacing as she escaped the greasy sheets. She filched one of Jock's cigarettes, hating the stale taste the minute she lit it. Their room was a royal mess. Open books piled on wrinkled, unwashed clothes, paper plates covered with the dried remains of pizza crusts and chinese noddles sitting on desk corners and on the top of their dresser, smelly beer cans scattered on chairs and littering the floor, scraps of paper strewn everywhere, with not a bare, uncluttered spot to be seen. A thick layer of dust covered everything. Enough was enough, she decided, stripping the blankets from the bed and ripping off the sheets. If she slept in that pit for one more night, she was bound to wake up the next morning with bedbugs. She stuffed the sheets into a pillowcase, tossed it in the closet, and rummaged through the linen shelf until she found a clean set.

Where the hell was Jock?

Forget about her; you're not her keeper, she told herself angrily, swiftly making the bed, absentmindedly creating tight girl guide corners she would kick out the minute she slid between them that night. She had hated girl guides, with all those smarmy moms so proud of their sweet little girls, with all the sweet little girls sucking up to get badges for doing asinine things. She returned to the closet for a garbage bag, and then furiously tossed in paper plates, beer cans, empty cigarette packs, the contents of overflowing ashtrays, crumpled pieces of paper and anything else which displeased her troubled eyes.

And what about that scheming, cheating lover of hers? Where had she been since the night her secret had been unveiled? Jo swooped in on the dead plant sitting on the grimy windowsill over Jock's bed and threw it into the bag, pot and all. Damn Blue. Making her suffer because she didn't have the discipline to resist temptation. Two-timing her without a second thought. Well, Jo would teach her a lesson or two about two-timing, although she hadn't made love with Jock with that specific purpose in mind. Or at least she didn't think she had.

And yes, where was that damn fool roommate of hers?

You do a favour for a friend, and look where it gets you, she raged, grabbing the two corners of the garbage bag and tying them together in a tight knot, opening the door and plopping it roughly on the floor, ignoring the loud crash of beer cans coming together forcefully. She slammed the door and retrieved the pillowcase from the closet, cramming dirty clothes on top of the sheets, indiscriminately mixing hers and Jock's. It was that damn woman's turn to do the laundry, but did Jock care? Did she even notice there was nothing clean in their dresser drawers or in the closet, and that Jo didn't have a decent thing to wear to class?

Maybe Jock had gone home.

The overflowing pillowcase tucked out of sight in the closet, Jo swiftly gathered the books and ring-binders scattered under the beds, on chair seats and on the floor and sorted through them, placing them in two neat piles on the desk, hers on one side, Jock's on the other.

Naw. She wouldn't run home to mommy and daddy. Not Jock. And as for Blue, she was probably out there screwing around with great abandon, celebrating her freedom now that Jo was no longer hanging around her neck like a heavy millstone. Well, damn the both of them!

She paused in her frantic housecleaning and looked around. Not bad. Too much dust, now swirling happily in the air, but not bad. She ran fingers through her hair, grimacing. It was high time to take care of herself. She opened the closet door and grabbed a bottle of shampoo, a bar of soap and her towel.

So if Jock wasn't here and she wasn't at home, where was she?

I didn't do anything wrong, Jo muttered to herself as she climbed into the shower and scrubbed her hair until her aching scalp protested. Jock wanted it too, so who could blame me for giving in? Blue, maybe. But who was she to complain? Glass houses and first stones to be thrown, etc. Now they were even. But where did that leave her? And Jock? She vigorously soaped her body and then rinsed it off, feeling clean for the first time in days. She, of all people, had started to smell! It was so stupid to let herself go over such a little thing. As if having sex with your best friend was a little thing, especially when your best friend was in love with you and you were in love with somebody else. As if both your lover and your best friend dropping out of sight was a little thing. Not that she had tried to call Blue. That would have been a sign of weakness, and besides, it was all Blue's fault, so Blue should be the one to apologize. Well, maybe skipping classes all week was a little thing; she was so agitated that she couldn't tell.

This is your conscience speaking, she whispered mockingly, closing the taps and wrapping herself in her towel. She got out and used the palm of her hand to clear a spot in the steam-covered mirror. She looked seedy; her complexion was mottled, her eyes red-rimmed, her cheeks deflated, her lips pale and thin. She sneered at her reflection and let the mirror cloud up again, relieved when her image fogged.

If only her brain would do the same thing. And her imagination. She hadn't worried when Jock hadn't come back that night; after all, their first encounter since they made love was bound to be embarrassing, and Jock wasn't highly skilled in the social graces. But when a second night came and went and Tony had knocked on the door looking for Jock, she had suddenly lost her complacency.

Where was she, anyway? Staying away to make Jo worry?

She hurried back to their room, but it was as deserted as when she had left it. There were no new cigarette butts in the ashtray, no recently emptied beer cans by the side of Jock's bed. The books were still piled neatly on opposite sides of the desk, unopened, neglected. The room even smelled quiet. Only the dust had been active while she was in the shower, settling on every surface like snow gently falling to earth on a windless day.

It had been three days now. She would have to call Jock's mother, and even then, what could she say? Hi, I'm worried about Jock, she hasn't been home all week? Is she by any chance there? And what if she wasn't? What if she had well and truly disappeared?

Jo had lost control of the situation. She was an intelligent, take-charge person, but that meant nothing now, not when Blue was probably with Suzanne, not when Jock might be lost and in trouble. She was upset. And having to wear a mismatched pair of jeans and sweater to class because Jock hadn't bothered do the laundry upset her further.

The door creaked. Jo spun around.

"Hi."

Being meek would get her nowhere. Neither would being reasonable. "Where the hell have you been?"

"Around," Jock replied with a shrug.

"Around?"

"What have you done to the room?"

Jo watched her walk to her unmade bed and sit down.

"I cleaned it up. You know, cleaned? C-L-E-A-N-E-D, as in changing my sheets, doing the garbage — "

"Oh, give me a break," Jock interrupted.

"Give *you* a break! How could you go off without a word like that? Do you know how worried I was?"

"You sound like my mother," Jock said with a titter. "Is there any beer?"

"No, there isn't any beer. And anyway, you drink too much," Jo responded.

"My mother for sure," Jock replied disparagingly, lying down, then turning on her side to face the wall.

"Haven't you got anything to say for yourself?" Jo said, hating the plaintive whine evident in her voice. Had she stooped to begging? Her? With Jock?

"Guess not," Jock answered sleepily.

It was all too much. Jo marched over to Jock's bed, grasped her shoulder and shook her.

"Hey!"

"At least have the common decency to tell me where you were," Jo raged.

"Like you always tell me where you've been? Or where you're going? And who with?" Jock replied angrily, turning around and sitting up.

Jo opened her mouth to reply and then realized that she had no right to say anything. How many nights had she stayed over at Blue's without calling Jock to say she wouldn't be home?

"Exactly! So why do I owe you an explanation?" Jock asked, getting up and pulling a cigarette from the pack in her pocket, flicking her lighter and taking a deep drag.

"But I was worried — " Jo began uncertainly.

"So?"

Who was this woman, anyway? Standing there in front of Jo, she looked taller, more mature, even older. Part best friend, part stranger. And her eyes were inquisitive, evaluating Jo's increasing confusion with a new and very disconcerting wisdom.

Jock suddenly laughed. "What can I say? Look, I guess there's no point in playing games."

"No," Jo said in a quiet voice.

"I called someone I met at the bar."

"And you went to her place."

"Yes."

"And spent three days there."

"Yes."

"And three nights."

"Well, yes," Jock replied, unable to hide the smugness in her voice.

"I see," Jo replied. She should be happy for Jock. And didn't this solve most of her problems, relieve her of the guilt of not being sure whether she had used Jock to get back at Blue? So why did she feel this numbness, this ache in the pit of her stomach?

"Hey, you were the one who encouraged me to go out and get laid," Jock reminded her, snuffing out her cigarette in the clean ashtray.

"I know," Jo replied, wandering away. "I know."

Silence descended like a cold winter's night. Jo heard Jock light another cigarette and inhale sharply, then the squeak of the spongy springs as Jock sat back down on her bed.

"I was worried, that was all," Jo said lamely, opening a book at random. It was Jock's first year calculus text, and it made about as much sense as the way she felt.

The bed squeaked again and Jo felt Jock's hands grasp her shoulders. "I'm sorry." Jock's lips grazed the back of her neck, making her shiver. She turned around and they kissed as if it was the most natural thing in the world to do, as if Jock had not just returned from three days and nights in another woman's bed, as if Jo had not spent those three days and nights enraged, worried and confused.

"Well isn't this an interesting little domestic scene."

Jo broke away from Jock's embrace. "Blue!"

"You know, you should make sure your door is locked before you partake," Blue commented laconically, her thin body in a state of apparent relaxation as she leaned against the closed door, an amused smile turning up the corners of her lips. "Otherwise you might find yourselves on the carpet and summarily expelled from this fair institution of ours for indulging in unnatural acts, as they so quaintly still call it."

She was stalling for time to regain her composure, Jo realized suddenly. Her smile, her casualness, they were just a front to hide her real feelings.

"Thanks, I'll remember that," Jock replied, her voice cool.

"Blue, I — "

"You two must have a lot to talk about, so I think I'll go see how Tony's doing," Jock interrupted.

"Why bother? It appears that you're already part of the family, so why not hang around and enjoy the fun?" Blue suggested coolly.

"No, thanks," Jock replied.

"Got better things to do?"

"Undoubtedly." And with that, Jock slid her cigarette pack into her pocket and walked stiffly to the door, stopping directly in front of Blue. "Do you mind?"

"Why should I?" Blue answered, stepping aside and opening the door.

"I thought not," Jock retorted with a glare. She stepped over the doorframe and the two women stared stonily at each other for a split second.

Ouch! Jo watched Blue give Jock one of her superior smiles and then close the door in her face. Double ouch! The two of them might not have been capable of being friends, but it looked like they were going to make quite spectacular enemies!

"So."

"You didn't have to treat her like that," Jo said.

"Don't change the subject."

Jo shrugged and turned away from the displeasure etched on Blue's face. So what if she had been caught in the act? So had Blue, in a manner of speaking. And at least Jock was a friend, not a total stranger like Suzanne. And at least she wasn't obsessed with Jock, not like Blue was with Suzanne.

"So while the cat's away, and all that," Blue said lightly, moving away from the door and into the room.

Jo shrugged again. She would be damned if she was going to let Blue make her feel guilty, because she wasn't!

"Please, Jo, talk to me," Blue exclaimed harshly, her hands spinning Jo around to face her.

"I haven't done anything wrong," Jo retorted.

"You mean to tell me that — "

"I mean to tell you just that," Jo interrupted. "And you have no right to come here and put me through an inquisition, not after what you've done."

Blue laughed and released her hold on Jo's shoulders. "You're right, of course. I was wrong. I shouldn't have got involved with Suzanne, and once I did, I should have told you about it right away. But I didn't, and I'm sorry."

"Well, that's something," Jo conceded gracelessly.

"And I haven't seen her since. Or anyone else," Blue added.

"Oh." So much for all her vivid imaginings of that sacrilegious triad, of Blue and Suzanne and the dildo, or of Blue branching out and carnally enjoying her new-found freedom with every lesbian in town.

"I wanted some time to think," Blue continued. "About me. And about us."

"Oh." While she was in bed with Jock and then worrying that Jock had wandered off in despair, Blue had been in a profound state of introspection about their relationship. And Jock had been in bed with another woman. How ironic. How stupid.

"But maybe I took too much time doing all that thinking," Blue said sarcastically.

"Well, why didn't you tell me? I thought we were through, that you had gone back to Suzanne!"

"For a little consolation?" Blue asked harshly. "Well, now I wish I had."

"Oh!" Jo exclaimed, frustrated.

"The two of you have been fooling around, huh?" Blue asked, her tone casual, her eyes bitter.

Jo turned her head.

"Having some fun while I sweated it out," Blue added.

"It wasn't like that," Jo responded helplessly.

"I bet."

How had she arrived at this impasse? She looked at Blue, who was deep in thought, her expression dour. Why on earth had she believed that she could escape the consequences of sexual involvement with Jock? Wasn't one woman at a time enough? But when she had slept with Jock, she hadn't been certain that she still wanted Blue, or that Blue was available even if she did. She had been angry, hurt. She had wanted to get back at Blue. But she hadn't used Jock for that, she *hadn't*! What had happened with Jock was separate, in a category by itself. Or was it?

"Well, maybe I'd better do some more thinking," Blue said finally, sounding defeated.

"Blue, you know how these things happen. Jock is just an old friend," Jo said, trying to reassure her. And it was true, although she was at a loss to explain why such a sudden and powerful attraction had arisen between them once they had taken the first step, once they had kissed, undressed, touched, come together. Something in their relationship had changed, and it wasn't a subtle alteration, one which could be erased from her memory or easily ignored.

"Yeah, well, here's something else for you to think about: old friends sometimes make the best lovers," Blue said softly.

"No," Jo responded, backing off.

"Oh, yes. And don't tell me it didn't feel good. You've known each other for years. Probably the only thing you hadn't done together was sex," she stated baldly.

It was true. They were soul buddies. When babies, they had napped in the same beds, and everybody, including their mothers, had waxed poetic about how cute they looked together. As toddlers, they had competed bitterly, their harrowing antagonism not touching the strength of their attachment to each other. As children, they had ruled the neighbourhood, trading on an unquestioned loyalty which kept them together when all the other kids changed sides as thoughtlessly as they changed socks. As teenagers, they had shared secrets, the intimacy of the locker room, the gradual knowledge that they were different, that they preferred women. They had even cuddled up in the same sleeping bag when they had camped out in Jock's tent on cold summer nights. They had the same roots, a common history. She knew the shape, texture and smell Jock's body almost as well as she knew her own. This realization was devastating. How, after all these years, could she have been so foolish to take that one, last step? To complete the circle? And what did it mean now that it was complete?

"You see what I mean," Blue said, her tone fatalistic.

"Yes," Jo whispered. "Yes, I do."

Blue sighed. "So what do you want to do?"

"How should I know?" Jo retorted, angry with herself, Blue, Jock, the world.

Blue chuckled wearily. "I had hoped you might."

"Well, I don't," Jo replied, her anger suddenly spent. None of this was Blue's fault. Blue had just been herself, no better, no worse. Her obsession with Suzanne had nothing to do with Jo. Jo understand this now, because her relationship with Jock had nothing much to do with how she felt about Blue. That hadn't changed. She still loved her. But it was infinitely more complicated now, because she hadn't yet sorted out how she felt about Jock.

"Call me," Blue said, opening the door.

"Don't go," Jo replied, panicking.

"I have to," Blue responded, and then she left.

I can't stay here alone, Jo thought when the door closed quietly behind Blue. I just can't. I know, I'll go to class. She gathered up her briefcase and her winter coat and ran from the room. If she listened carefully and concentrated hard on taking notes, she could probably distract herself. Still, it was too bad she was incapable of leaving her tangled thoughts behind with the dust she had never got around to wiping up.

# Muted Memories

So where were they planning to ship her now, Oats wondered, staring stolidly at the uniformed bearer of bad news. "We're releasing you today," the nurse had said, and panic had immediately welled up in Oats' gut. Where am I going to go, she had wanted to wail. But she had kept her mouth shut; it was no good ranting and raving. After all, she had a family here in Montreal and the hospital knew it, although she would rather have died from the heart attack than go home to mother.

Well, not really. Almost, but not quite. But it would never work. Her mother was too old, and had been since she was young. A perpetual complainer, always worried that the house would get dirty if anybody attempted to really live in it, and always preoccupied about the state of her health for no good reason, since she was strong as an ox and always had been. Oats and her brother had fended for themselves and eventually each other when they were sick, learning at a remarkably young age that their mother was so worried about catching what they had that she went near them only if their illnesses were deemed life-threatening, which kid's diseases seldom were, in those days at least. So going home to mother would be like going home to her empty apartment; her mother would suddenly begin to live the social life of a debutante or shop until she dropped, even though it would be far less exhausting to take care of Oats. Not that she didn't love her mother; she did, but from a distance. At close quarters, they chaffed. There was always a short honeymoon, half an hour at most, when they worked hard at convincing themselves and each other that it would be different this time. After all, there had been so much water under the bridge that all the old antagonisms must have died from neglect, right? Wrong. Honeymoon over, disagreements would raise their ugly little heads, dislike would smoulder and burst into flames, searing them with its heat and more often than not, forcing a dishonourable retreat on both sides.

"All your papers will be ready later this morning," the nurse continued, oblivious to Oats' growing dismay. "And someone will be around with your prescription and instructions on how to take your medication."

"Fine," Oats croaked.

The nurse gave her an impersonal smile, added a dismissive nod of the head and swept from the room.

"Lucky you," commented Doris, her new roommate, as she slowly pulled herself to a sitting position. "I haven't even had my operation yet."

"But I don't know where I'm going to go," Oats mumbled, swiping at a stray tear as it escaped from her eye and tickled her cheek.

"Your family?" suggested Doris, a chatty, down-to-earth woman with a biting sense of humour who was shortly going to lose a second breast to cancer. Oats liked her, and they had quickly established a comfortable relationship.

"My mother hates sick people," Oats replied dryly.

"A friend's, then," Doris said helpfully.

"Maybe," Oats said doubtfully. Oats wasn't oblivious to the failings of the women with whom she had surrounded herself. Most of her friends were of the fine-weather variety, buzzing around when Oats was at her best, willing to trail after her when she was bar hopping with great abandon or plotting some wacky adventure which would give them a thrill or scandalize them or provide them with a vicarious sense of danger or something to brag about for weeks to come. But they faded into the shadows when disaster hit, avoiding people in trouble. They were not in the least interested in hearing about things like hangovers, poverty, job loss, break-ups, gay-bashing, or growing old. Or illness. Most of them hadn't even come to visit.

"There's always a convalescent home," Doris said.

Could it really come to that? Being carted off to a place for people who had nowhere else to go and no one to look after them? For people nobody cared about? No way. She would rather go home and crawl from bed to bathroom to kitchen than face the ignominy of a convalescent home. But what was she going to do for cash? Fred, her boss, was holding her job open, but the amount of money she was collecting on unemployment insurance was barely enough to cover the rent and her car payments. She didn't have a cent left over for groceries, not to mention the phone bill, the gas bill, the hydro bill, food ...

"I'm sure you'll work it out," Doris reassured her.

"Yeah, me too," Oats responded, although she didn't know how.

"Good morning, campers!"

"You're in a good mood today," Oats said, begrudging Kate her habitual and rather disgusting tendency to wake up cheerful.

"It's not snowing, I didn't have to dig my car out, and there weren't any traffic jams," Kate announced. "Isn't that enough to be thankful for?"

"I guess so." And your bruises are fading, Oats thought. That's even more to be thankful for.

"Did you hear? She's going home today," Doris said to Kate.

"I sure did," Kate responded. "Isn't that great, Oats?"

"I guess so," Oats replied morosely.

"It's just that she's worried about where she's going to go," Doris confided rather apologetically to Kate.

"I know," Kate said with a nod. "Excuse us for a moment?"

"Sure," Doris replied, picking up a dog-eared paperback.

Kate pulled the curtain around Oats' bed and sat in the chair beside it.

"You're looking good," Oats commented.

"Better," Kate corrected her with a laugh. "Not good yet, but better. And I'm feeling better, too."

"I'm glad," Oats replied, reaching out and grasping Kate's hand.

"About your release — "

"Please don't let them send me to a convalescent home," Oats said swiftly. "I couldn't stand it."

"Shhh," Kate remonstrated gently, reassuringly squeezing Oats' hand. "Stop fretting. No one is going to send you to a convalescent home."

"But where am I going to go, then? I can't go home alone, I'm not strong enough. I've hardly been on my feet. And you know my mother," Oats added.

"You're going to Melba's," Kate said, a self-satisfied smile animating her face.

"Melba's?"

"Yes."

Oats stared at Kate, not daring to believe her.

"It's true."

"How did you get her to agree to that?" Oats asked, feeling a crying jag coming on. She had clung to the belief that Melba would eventually forgive her. And she had been certain that once she got her strength back, she would think of a way to prove to Melba that she loved her. But she hadn't ever permitted herself to hope that Melba would take care of her, not when she was so helpless. In her dreams it had happened, but real life was another matter. Melba didn't owe her a thing; in fact, it was the other way around, and Oats knew it.

"Oats, there's something you have to understand; Melba would do this for anyone. For a relative, a good friend, or an ex-lover," Kate carefully explained.

"She told you that?" Oats asked slowly.

"Yes. We had dinner the other night," Kate replied. "She is still angry with you, but she doesn't want her anger to interfere with what she feels is the right thing to do."

"So I shouldn't assume anything," Oats said disappointedly.

"No you shouldn't," Kate confirmed. "When you picked up that floozie and took her home, you changed everything."

"Floozie!" Oats said with a dull laugh. "I haven't heard that word for years! You're showing your age, Kate."

"Well, that's exactly what she was, wasn't she?" Kate continued, refusing to be baited. "You stuck your foot in your cunt, if you'll excuse my language, and made a fool of yourself. And not for the first time, I might add."

"Come on, Kate," Oats complained, squirming uncomfortably in her bed.

"It's true, and you know it," Kate continued persistently.

"Okay, okay, I know it," Oats admitted reluctantly. "But I paid for it, didn't I?"

"Paying for it is easy. Look, saying you're sorry isn't enough; you're always saying you're sorry, as if that makes any difference. Well, 'I'm sorry' isn't some magic incantation that makes it better or turns back the clock!" Kate said vehemently.

"Has Maxine been at you again?" Oats asked, suddenly understanding that this wasn't really about her at all.

"Yes. Yes she has. But I can handle it," Kate responded. "And eventually she'll stop and leave me alone. She hurt me, Oats. Just like you hurt Melba."

Oats began to protest, but Kate stopped her with a wave of her hand. "There a difference of degree, of course, and physical abuse crosses a line most of us think women never cross, but emotional abuse is wrong too. So I don't blame Melba for wanting out of your relationship, for not believing that you'll never do it again, just like I don't believe Maxine will never do it again."

Oats' immediate reaction was to reject what Kate had said out of hand, because raping and beating up on a woman were unspeakably vile, and she had never, ever considered stooping to that level. But she took a deep breath and forced herself to think about it. Was there a connection? Did it matter what caused the suffering? Could common variety cheating be classified with rape? With battering? If so, she had spent her whole life emotionally abusing women. "Kate, if you don't mind, I think that's too big a chunk for me to swallow right now," she responded weakly.

A look of brusque sympathy crossed Kate's face and then disappeared. "I understand," she replied dryly, standing up. "But do me a favour and don't forget what I said."

"I won't," Oats promised, her voice cracking.

"Melba will pick you up in an hour, so why don't you see if you can get dressed by yourself," Kate suggested, looking at her watch.

She nodded and watched Kate disappear around the side of the curtain. Everybody was mad at her, even her best friend. How had life turned so relentlessly sour in such a short period of time? But of course it's my own fault, she thought angrily. I've been acting like a fool, and Melba has paid the price. She eased herself out of bed, taking baby-steps across the floor, her arms stretched out horizontally for balance. The clothes in her locker were alien and although she vaguely recognized them, they were too big, hanging shapelessly on her frame. She must have lost weight. She packed her few belongings in her suitcase and sat on the bed, wanting a cigarette. Waiting had never been her strong point, especially when what she was waiting for was potentially unpleasant. How could she accept impersonal charity from a woman she was still in love with? Perhaps this was her punishment for acting the way she had, although she didn't believe that retribution fell only on those who deserved it. Life wasn't as cut and dried as all that. Lots of really nice people had horribly unfair things happen to them, like Doris, for example. She got up off the bed and opened the curtain.

"Ready?" Doris asked.

"As ready as I'll ever be," Oats responded with a smile.

"Well, good luck," Doris said, offering her hand.

"Thanks. I have a feeling I'll need it," Oats said, crossing the room to shake Doris' hand.

"Have you been waiting long?" Melba asked, rushing into the room.

"No. I just finished getting dressed," Oats replied. "Bye, then. I'm sure everything will go just fine," she said awkwardly to Doris.

Doris just smiled and nodded.

"Here I am," said the breathless attendant, pushing a wheelchair before him.

"I don't need that," Oats protested.

"Regulations, madame, regulations," he intoned, sounding bored.

Oats rolled her eyes and sat down. Melba picked up Oats' suitcase and they left the room, Melba walking beside the wheelchair. "What's the matter with her?" she asked as they moved slowly down the hall.

"Breast cancer," Oats answered.

"Ah."

There didn't seem like much to say after that, even when the attendant deposited Oats just inside the front door and left them alone. "Jeez, it's cold!" Oats exclaimed with a shiver once they were outside.

"Hospitals are always overheated," Melba replied, leading Oats to the parking lot.

"Yeah," Oats agreed politely, although she hadn't actually noticed. The heater in Melba's car immediately began to emit gusts of hot air, and Oats was dozing by the time Melba pulled into her building's underground parking lot.

"We're here," Melba announced, turning the key in the ignition. The merciful warmth swiftly disappeared when she opened the door, and Oats woke up. Her bones felt stiff and tired, but she unfolded herself from the car seat and waited for Melba to retrieve her suitcase from the trunk.

"You live here?" she asked as they rode the elevator to the fourteenth floor. Oats hated elevators. She was sure they were lying in wait to pounce on claustrophobic souls who had entrusted their lives to the whims of a couple of thin, probably frayed wires, to door mechanisms which worked when they felt like it, to Hydro Quebec's regular system failures.

"Yes," Melba replied with an unreadable smile. She unlocked the door and ushered Oats into a small apartment. "I'm afraid there's only one bedroom," Melba added. The sofa-bed was open and made up, the cheerful red bedspread the only bright spot in the whole room.

"That's fine," Oats said, sitting heavily on the bed. She felt exhausted; it was scary to be so weak.

"I have to get back to work," Melba said, hovering just inside the open door.

"I understand," Oats replied.

"You look like you could use a nap."

"That's exactly what I'm going to do," Oats said with false cheerfulness, wishing Melba would go. Their polite conversation was so painful that she would rather be alone.

"There's food in fridge when you wake up," Melba said, approaching the sofa.

"Fine."

"And we'll pick up some of your clothes tomorrow," Melba added.

"Great."

"I'm off, then."

So go, Oats urged. Before I scream out loud.

"Will you be all right?"

"Yes."

"Do you have your pills?"

"Yes."

"There's water in the fridge."

"Good."

"See you later."

"Okay," Oats said without enthusiasm. Would she never, ever go? Melba turned away.

"Melba?"

"Yes?"

"Thanks," Oats said.

"Don't. Just don't," Melba whispered, walking swiftly across the room and out the door.

Okay, so I won't, Oats thought silently as the door closed. She placed her head on the pillow, squeezed her eyes shut and began to listen to the silence.

# Silent Night

"**Y**ou did what?" Tony whispered so loudly that students in the front of the auditorium turned their heads.

"Shhh! Do you want the prof to notice you, for god's sake?" Jock said, raising her textbook and ducking behind it.

"Well, yes, actually. Maybe he'll give me some points for showing up once in awhile," Tony replied.

Nerd. Jock put her book down, covering the hetero graffiti carved on its grimy top. She should make an effort and take some notes. The problem was that she had skipped so many classes that she no longer had any idea what the prof was talking about.

"Anyway, what did you say you did?" Tony asked in a quieter voice.

"You heard me," Jock said impatiently, straining to catch the question the prof was asking. He never called on people in the back row, assuming that they were neither listening nor prepared, but it was better to be vigilant; teachers were like snakes — they struck when you least expected it.

"Let's get out of here and go for a coffee," Tony suggested, closing her book.

"Would you please shut up?" hissed the man sitting next to them. "I can't hear what he's saying."

"Then move up front," Tony snarled. "Come on, Jock, let's go."

Why not? She was going to fail this course anyway; she would cram at the last minute to make her failure a more respectable one, but what point was there in sitting in an uncomfortable chair listening to an incomprehensible lecture and trying to copy meaningless hieroglyphics from the blackboard? Jock closed her book and slid it into her briefcase. "Okay. Let's go."

They scurried from the room, coats and briefcases in hand, and walked out into the early evening. Their booted feet plowed through the slush, following the well-trodden path to the student union building. It didn't matter that they had left before the class was over, Jock decided. She couldn't do any worse than she already was, and the prof probably didn't recognize her anyway. She felt depressed. She hated winter with a passion, especially the short days. When it was dark by four-thirty in the afternoon, all she wanted to do was curl up and hibernate. And she didn't like calculus or physics or biology or any of that stuff you had to memorize ad nauseam. If she didn't flunk out altogether, she would change her major next year and do computer science or psychology or even english.

"Tell me again," Tony urged once they had lined up for coffee and donuts and sat down at an empty table in the corner.

"Jo and I slept together. And then I went over to Candy's and spent three days there," Jock replied, brushing crumbs from the table top and then pouring milk and sugar into her coffee, stirring it with a plastic spoon.

"Who is Candy? You never told me about her. And how come you went to her place for three whole days?"

"What do you think?" Jock replied impatiently, taking a bite of her sugar donut.

"You mean — "

"Yeah, yeah, that's exactly what I mean," Jock said. She had gone with Candy because she had been terrified of how she felt about Jo, but being with Candy had made things worse, not better. She hadn't been able to put Jo out of her mind even when she had been making love with Candy. Oh sure, she knew about sex now; drunk or sober, Candy had been a good teacher. And it had been fun, if that was all you were looking for. Candy liked sex, she liked booze, and maybe she even liked Jock, but she had never said so. And when Jock had woke up that final morning, she had felt disgusted with Candy and with herself. So she had made a few pitiful excuses, dressed and gone back to the dorm, feeling nervous, guilty and frightened.

"I don't believe it," Tony said, cramming half her jelly donut into her mouth.

"I don't care what you believe," Jock retorted. "It happens to be the truth."

"Huh," Tony huffed, her mouth too full of donut to reply.

Jock lit a cigarette and sipped her coffee. Tony was just jealous, but it didn't matter. Actually, she wasn't sure if anything mattered much any more. Either that, or it all mattered too much. She was too confused to know. And too much in love. But she couldn't compete with Blue, match Jo's maturity, or deal with her own insecurities.

"Anyway, you're crazy," Tony finally said, biting off another chunk of donut.

"So tell me something I don't already know," Jock retorted, her appetite suddenly disappearing. "Here, you can have mine," she said, shoving her half-eaten donut across the table.

"Thanks," Tony gulped, washing the rest of her donut down with coffee.

"Look, I don't really want to talk about it, okay?" Jock said, finishing her cigarette.

"They why did you bring it up?" Tony responded with impeccable logic, biting into Jock's donut. Cherry filling oozed out and dropped to the tray.

Jock shrugged. She had to tell somebody. To see what it sounded like when said aloud. To make it real. "How should I know?"

"This is the most pointless conversation I've ever had," Tony complained.

"Go back to class, then," Jock said, annoyed. She rose from her chair and pulled her coat on.

"Where are you going?"

"I don't know. Back to the dorm, maybe," Jock replied, buttoning her coat.

"To see Jo?"

"Maybe. Maybe not."

Perhaps she should do something different, like go to the library and study. Or ride the subway downtown and take in a movie. She felt like too much of a pariah to go back to her room, for what she hadn't mentioned to Tony was that Jo wasn't talking to her. And what a miserable existence that was, waking up and facing the morning without their habitual chit-chat, spending the cold, snowy days avoiding their room and then coming in late and going to bed with her body shaking with silent tears once the lights were out.

Why wouldn't Jo talk to her, she wondered for the millionth time as she walked across campus, heading for St-Denis Street and the bars. Was she back with Blue and under strick orders to keep away? Was she angry because Jock had been with Candy? But that didn't make sense. Actually, none of if made any sense, so what good did it do to dwell on it?

"Hey, lover!" Candy exclaimed as Jock walked into the bar, tossing her coat on a vacant stool. "A beer for my woman!" she called to the bartender.

116

Already spiffed, Jock thought stolidly, suffering in silence as Candy draped herself over her shoulder in full view of the small crowd of women sitting in isolated pockets in corners of the bar. It was only Tuesday, so this was probably the most action they were going to see all night. "I haven't got a penny," she whispered in Candy's ear, although that wasn't exactly true. She had a few dollars in her pants pocket, but she was reluctant to spend it on beer.

"I'm paying," Candy announced, abruptly pulling away and tossing a crumpled twenty dollar bill on the glistening counter.

"Thanks."

"Where have you been, sweetie? I've been searching high and low for you," Candy told her, carelessly picking up three beer bottles by their necks and weaving her way to the back of the bar.

Jock grinned uncomfortably at the bartender and followed Candy, fully expecting the dangling bottles to crash to the floor at any moment, although they didn't.

"This is Sheila, my very best friend," Candy said, plopping the bottles on the wet table top.

"She always says that when she's had a wee bit too much," replied Sheila with a casual wave.

"And she always agrees," Candy laughed boisterously. "Sit down, why don't you?"

"Yeah, take a load off," joked Sheila.

Great, Jock thought. Just what she needed, two loaded dykes. They must have been waiting in line for the bar to open. But she sat, picked up her beer bottle and took a long drink. Maybe she could catch up with them if she hurried, especially if Candy was going to spring for the beer.

"So what do you think?" Candy asked.

Jock slowly lowered the bottle, looking from Candy to Sheila, who was staring at her.

"Not bad, not bad," Sheila commented.

"I told you she was real cute," Candy confided.

Hey, what was this, a meat market? Jock didn't know whether to laugh or get angry.

"After all, it's not every day you find yourself a virgin," Candy said drunkenly. Unfortunately, the jukebox was between songs, and heads turned. The blithering idiot, Jock thought; couldn't she keep her mouth shut? Even the walls probably turned to view this rare sight. Anger it was, then. And spite. And the urge to kill. "Well, thanks for the beer," she muttered, getting up. Jo's silent treatment would be preferable to this.

"But you're not finished," Candy protested, grasping her arm.

"Oh yes I am," Jock replied, wrenching her arm away and retrieving her coat from the nearby stool.

"Come on, don't be a party pooper," Candy whined, trailing along after Jock.

"Sorry, but I've got a hot date," Jock lied.

"Hey, you aren't going to leave me alone, are you?"

"You're not alone, you've got your best friend Sheila to keep you company," Jock retorted.

"You know what I mean," Candy answered with a suggestive leer.

"I'm late," Jock replied, feigning a glance at her watch. It was only seven and her heart sank; she had hours to waste before she could safely return home.

"So go. I don't care," Candy said, her mood abruptly changing. "You were a lousy lay, anyway."

Jock's tender ego swiftly deflated. It's just another thing which doesn't matter, she told herself, leaving the bar and taking a deep breath of cold air. Candy was drunk; she probably didn't know what she was saying. Still, what a disaster! Jock hunched her shoulders to fend off the wind and walked down the street, slowing climbing the stairs to Ruff.

She was forced to spend every cent in her pocket to buy a beer, which she nursed slowly, sitting on a stool at the bar, letting the loud music wash over her. It was all so useless. She was going to fail nearly every one of her courses, and she didn't care. No, that wasn't true. She cared desperately, but she couldn't do anything about it. It was too late, she had missed too many lectures, and she was too far behind. Failure had somehow overtaken her while she had been preoccupied with other things, with smoking and drinking and looking for love and trying not to feel like an alien from another planet among all the eggheads and super dykes and people who knew so much more than she did.

And then she had gone to bed with a woman she didn't know, a woman who started to drink after lunch and who was somehow still able to perform sexually come nightfall. This lurching, spasmodic sex, this selfish taking on both sides, this elevator ride where Candy's moods had changed for no apparent reason had left Jock with more questions than answers. She hadn't been able to relax for three days and nights, to permit herself the luxury of feeling good about what was happening. She felt uncomfortable, out of her element. Candy had been an experience all right, but one she didn't particularly want to repeat. Not that another invitation would be forthcoming, not after tonight, she thought with an involuntary snicker.

"Ready for another?"

Oh no. Not Blue. "I haven't got enough money left," Jock replied, slowly turning her head.

"So you'll owe me," Blue said lightly, gesturing to the bartender as she sat down beside Jock.

Oh, great. What was she going to do now? But Jock accepted the frosty beer bottle, taking a drink as she watched the bartender remove her empty glass and wipe the counter.

"I thought you'd be home wallowing in domestic bliss," Blue said.

"Are you kidding?" she blurted, immediately chagrined when Blue's eyebrows shot up.

"Sorry I asked," Blue replied, and to Jock's relief, she left it at that. They drank silently but not companionably, although Jock was too distraught to care.

"Well, I'm off," Blue said, draining her bottle and standing up.

"Blue, wait," Jock said impulsively.

"What?"

"Look, maybe I shouldn't say this, but I don't know what's going on with Jo," Jock confessed.

Blue sat down again. "That makes two of us."

"What?"

Blue waved her empty bottle at the bartender and paid for two more beers. "She isn't talking to me."

"Me neither."

"Well I'll be damned ... "

They stared at each other and then looked away, Blue to lift her bottle and drink, Jock to light a cigarette. Jock felt sorry for Blue, but most of all, she felt sorry for herself. Jo was an enigma. She always had been an independent cuss, even in high school, going her own way no matter what, while Jock had followed the crowd in her own boisterous, meandering fashion. Jo always knew what she wanted, Jock rarely, because she hadn't bothered to take time to think about it. Plus ça change ...

"Is she always like this?" Blue asked.

"I don't know," Jock admitted.

"But you've known her all your life," Blue replied with no little disbelief.

If anybody had asked that question two weeks ago, Jock would have said that of course she knew Jo, but that had obviously been an illusion. She was beginning to understand that Jo gave people precisely what they wanted, but when push came to shove, she took it all back, as if it hadn't meant a thing. "Jo's got a mind of her own," she said glumly.

"Obviously," Blue said, sounding amused. "That's one reason I like her."

They were operating on difference wave lengths, Jock thought. Her depression deepened. How could she compete with a woman like this?

"Do you know why she isn't talking to you?" Blue asked carefully.

"No."

"Me neither."

So there it was. Both of them in love with Jo, both of them ready to apply for membership in the walking wounded club. What a laugh. "I've got to go," Jock said, abysmally tired of the whole thing. "Thanks for the beer."

"Sure," Blue replied absently. Jock rose from the barstool and went outside. It was snowing. Again. And cold. Still. But Jock was broke, so there was no question of taking a cab back to the dorm, where the emotional temperature inside the room she shared with Jo would probably be colder than outside in the storm. Maybe she should stand there and let herself freeze to death.

"Jock!"

It was Blue again, her leather jacket unzipped, flapping in the gusting wind. "Want to have coffee at my place?"

Anything would be better than having to choose between dying from exposure or facing Jo's impenetrable silence. Or having to think one more wretched, solitary thought. Jock nodded and followed Blue to the bus stop.

# Spilled Beer

"**W**hat on earth am I doing here?" Kate said plaintively, grasping the sleeve of Melba's coat.

"It'll be all right. Come on, let's check our coats," Melba replied, leading Kate to the coat check, helping her off with her coat and handing it to the woman behind the counter. She didn't want Kate to have time to fret, to worry that it had been a mistake to come to l'Entr'acte.

"Melba, I want to go home," Kate said urgently.

"It's okay," Melba reassured her. "I'm sure you'll feel fine once we get inside." But she was beginning to feel anxious, probably because she was identifying so strongly with Kate's nervousness. She could tell that Kate wanted to bolt, to run from the bar and from her fears and hide behind the securely bolted locks on her apartment door.

"Melba — "

"Come on. Let's find a table," Melba said, taking Kate by the hand and walking briskly through the crowded bar, a false smile pasted on her face. She nodded to several women she knew, wondering whether this had been a wise move after all. They could have rented a video or just spent the evening talking, since Kate undoubtedly still needed to talk. But no, with the flawed wisdom of an armchair psychologist, Melba had decided that Kate should brave the waters. And a night on the town was one way to do it. Get out and about, be seen, return to the community in safe company. But somehow, it didn't feel right. Kate was too nervous. Maybe she wasn't ready yet.

"There's one," Melba said, rushing to claim it before someone else did.

"Phew, it's hot," Kate complained, wiping her brow.

"It's always hot," Melba replied, watching Kate nervously scan

121

the bar, looking for Maxine. What if Maxine was there? Melba didn't see her, but what if she came later? How would Kate feel? What would she do? Would Maxine make trouble? It was early, only ten, but the bar was already packed with overheated women on the prowl. It was a night to be out; miraculously, it hadn't snowed for a couple of days and the snowbanks had shrivelled to insignificance. The bare sidewalks were littered with salt which immediately stained boots white, and with sand which crackled grittily under-foot and insinuated itself into houses, hiding away in carpets and in the cracks between floor boards, refusing to surrender to the exhortations of even the most powerful vacuum cleaner.

"That was a nice dinner," Melba said once they had ordered mineral water. She would play the unaccustomed role of conver-sationalist to keep Kate's mind (and hers) off Maxine. Perhaps after awhile Kate would relax and begin to enjoy herself a little. After all, this was the one place in the world where they could be themselves, and Kate shouldn't have to give it up because of that wretched woman. And what if Maxine did show up? Melba tried to put that intrusive thought from her mind; after all, there was nothing she could do about it now. Either Maxine would come or she wouldn't, and if she did, they would deal with it then. "In fact, it was an incredible dinner," she added, looking at Kate.

"Yes, it was," Kate responded wanly, attempting to smile, her eyes darting repeatedly towards the front door.

"I really enjoy Greek food," Melba added helplessly, pausing to pay for her glass of mineral water, then pushing the lemon wedge into the glass. They had strolled along the restaurant strip on Prince Arthur Street, walking nearly to St-Louis Square before choosing a restaurant which had been packed with Friday-night diners from all over the city. They had ordered chicken brochettes, and then both of them had splurged on honey-filled baklava for dessert, followed by rich, strong coffee.

"Oats nearly had a fit," Melba said, making another attempt to distract Kate from her constant vigilance of front door.

"I bet," Kate responded, really looking at Melba for the first time since they had entered the bar.

"She couldn't believe that we would go out without her," Melba continued, encouraged by Kate's attention. She smiled, remember-ing the injured look on Oats' face when she broke the news, an expression which could not have been more tragic if she had just discovered that her lover had been unfaithful with another woman. It was probably the same pitiful expression Oats had displayed as a child when she had been deprived of something she wanted. Correction: of *anything* she wanted. Oats always took defeat personally; it was never brought about by circumstances beyond her control. And now that Oats was sick, everyone in the whole world was supposed to be sick, or at least to act like they were.

"What did she say?" Kate asked.

"Oh, that we should be ashamed of ourselves for gallivanting around and having a good time and leaving a nearly dead woman to fend for herself," Melba replied, laughing.

"Typical," Kate responded.

"And that nobody cared about her or about how she felt," Melba added.

Kate laughed and sipped her mineral water. "Silly girl."

"And how," Melba said emphatically. "I don't know why I put up with her."

"Do you want me to take her?" Kate asked at once. "I've got space."

Melba looked up, her levity suddenly gone. Sure, she could whisk Oats out the door and over to Kate's, lock, stock and barrel, and that would be that. It would be over, the circle broken, and she would be able to go on with her life believing that she had done her fair share. But would it really be over? And what life did she have to go on with? That meaningless nine to five existence, with work her only reason for living? Some reason; it was more like an excuse, and a barren one at that. "No. I have to work my way through this," she replied finally. "You understand."

"Yes, I do," Kate nodded, and Melba could see that she did. She understood that Melba was tempted, because Oats was not easy to love or to live with. It was difficult for any of their friends to picture them together, with Oats continuously dissembling while Melba proceeded carefully, methodically, logically. And they were both headstrong, absolutely certain they were proceeding in the right direction.

Kate shook her head and smiled.

"What?"

"I was just thinking that I've never met two people who were more different," Kate replied.

"How right you are," Melba answered. "Anyway, cheers."

"Cheers," Kate echoed, and they touched glasses and drank.
"Hi, Kate."

Kate looked up, her expression full of fear. But it was only Jo, hovering uncertainly over their table.

"Oh, hello, Jo. Do you know Melba?" Kate responded.

"I've seen you around," Melba said, shaking hands with the younger woman while keeping her eyes on Kate. Damn; she was going to turn into a nervous wreck if she didn't stop worrying about Maxine.

"Me too," Jo replied. "Anyway, I just thought I'd say hi."

"Are you alone? Want to join us?" Kate asked.

"Okay," Jo said, sitting down at once. "I hope I'm not interrupting anything," she added, putting her glass and beer bottle on the table.

"Not at all," Melba said heartily, hating the falseness in her voice. She shouldn't be so wary of these young things, but the trouble was that they never seemed to contribute anything useful to the conversation. Perhaps that was ageist, but it was certainly how she felt. Which was no excuse, she thought guiltily.

"So how is Oats?" Jo asked, playing with her beer bottle.

"Sue is recovering at home," Melba said primly, grimacing when she saw Kate smile. It was actually more like pacing the floor, a restless lion confined in a too-small cage.

"Is she going to be okay?" Jo asked self-consciously.

"Oh, yes," Melba replied lightly, not wanting to discuss Oats' private affairs with a near-stranger.

"I guess it takes time," Jo said, putting down her glass.

Melba arranged a smile on her face and nodded her head to the pounding music. Kate was pale, obviously nervous, but there was nothing Melba could do to counteract it, not with Jo there. It was too bad she didn't recognize anyone else; if she could gather a crowd around their table, Kate would feel more secure.

"Oh my god, Melba, it's Maxine!" Kate exclaimed.

Both Melba and Jo turned and looked toward the door. "It's all right, Kate. She can't do anything here," Melba said reassuringly, reaching out and grasping Melba's clammy hand in her own as she watched Maxine saunter through the crowd, stopping at the bar to buy a beer.

The three of them were motionless in an ocean of movement, like corpses on a battlefield where the war is still raging. Maxine stopped suddenly when she saw Kate and then moved inexorably toward them. Melba squeezed Kate's hand and carefully watched Maxine as she loomed over the table, ready to move at the least hint of violence. Maxine wasn't stupid enough to create a scene in the middle of the bar, was she?

"So," Maxine said, slamming her beer bottle on the table with such force that suds foamed over the rim, ran down the side and bubbled over the table. Several women at neighbouring tables glanced at them and then studiously looked away.

"Leave us alone," Melba said harshly, tightening her grasp on Kate's hand, trying to control the fear which was making her mouth dry. Maxine wouldn't. Not in a crowded bar. She couldn't possibly be that stupid, that much out of control.

"I want to have a little chat with you," Maxine said, ignoring Melba and speaking directly to Kate. "In private."

"Leave me alone," Kate replied, pulling her trembling hand from Melba's and standing up.

"I said privately," Maxine continued, weaving drunkenly.

Melba shot up so swiftly that her chair overturned, crashing against a woman seated at the table behind her.

"Hey! Watch it!"

"Sorry," Melba replied evenly, reaching back and straightening her chair without taking her eyes from Maxine.

"Come on," Maxine commanded, putting out her hand.

Kate reached down, picked up Maxine's beer bottle and swiftly emptied its contents into her outstretched hand.

Jo rose slowly, her mouth open, and backed away. By now the women sitting at the surrounding tables had realized that something extraordinary was happening; conversation had stopped, and they were all sitting on the edge of their chairs, ready to move out of the way.

"Is there a problem here?" asked one of the waitresses, staring at Maxine's dripping hand and the beer-covered table top.

"No, she just spilled her beer," Melba replied swiftly.

The waitress looked at Melba, then at Maxine. "Why don't you get a rag from the bar and clean this up before the floor gets all sticky?"

But Maxine didn't move. Melba's throat was parched; she desperately wanted a drink of water, but she was afraid that if she moved, she would break the motionless spell which enveloped them.

The waitress looked puzzled. "What's the matter with her?" No one replied.

Maxine looked so stupefied standing there with beer drying on her outstretched hand like a mustard glaze thickening on a ham roast that Kate started to laugh.

"You'd think no one ever spilled their beer before," the waitress grumbled as Maxine turned and stalked from the bar without another word, swiftly disappearing from view in the crowd of milling women.

"Yes, wouldn't you?" Melba replied with a disarming smile. "Why don't you bring me a glass of white wine? I feel like celebrating."

"I think I'd better have a mineral water," Jo said shakily.

"Well, I'm all for celebrating, so this time bring me a mineral water with *two* wedges of lemon," Kate joked.

They laughed and sat down, all talking at once, but not about Maxine. No, never about Maxine; they discussed the music, what the dancers were wearing, how awfully hot the bar was and wasn't the weather terrible this winter. Nothing was said about Maxine and what had happened. And eventually, Jo switched back to beer, Melba ordered another glass of white wine, and Kate continued her celebration with a second glass of mineral water with two lemon wedges.

# Free To Love

**M**y problems are nothing, Jo told herself, wiping wet, heavy snow from her shoulders. Not compared to Kate's. Look what she's lived through. And look at Oats, her whole life turned upside down by a heart attack. No, my problems are minuscule compared to theirs.

Except who did she love? Nothing had prepared her for this crisis. Coming out had been easy; one summer morning when she had been fourteen she woke up, and with thoughtful clarity, realized that she was a lesbian, something she cheerfully accepted before she got out of bed. That others might not be so accepting of her lesbianism was a safe assumption, given the social and political climate and the fact that she lived in a small, rather insular and conservative town, so she hadn't mentioned this discovery of hers, content to spend time in solitary exploration of this new and somewhat startling revelation.

Who was she? What did it mean that she was attracted to women? How did lesbians live? And where could she meet some? She had speculated about classmates, giving her own special interpretation to certain looks, gestures, tones of voice, special interests, hobbies, friendships, crushes, romantic inclinations. Some, like Jock and Tony, were clearly lesbians, while others were not so obvious. It had been like a private game of chance, although the stakes had been high, especially when she was perpetually horny and when her crushes on certain teachers and classmates had threatened to overwhelm her and make her do something premature, something stupid. She had not wanted to move too soon, before she was ready, before she knew for certain.

She had been so indecisive. Had spent so much time quibbling about such minor problems. Had lived through so many periods of intense teenage angst. When she thought of it now, which she rarely did, it seemed like nothing. That had been before, and this was after. "Before" accounted for most of her life, those arid, pre-sexual years when success was measured in high marks in school, in being the best player on winning teams, in being popular, in establishing peaceful co-existence with parents and siblings, in confirming that straight sex sucked. And "after," oh yes, *after*! She had grown up, left home, become a woman. She had discovered the power of good sex, lost her real virginity to an older woman, met Blue and fell in love. It had seemed so easy at the time.

Blue was her first real love. She was a little older, a lot more experienced, open to experimentation, somewhat of an anarchist, much too secretive and prickly as a porcupine, although she would rather die than admit it. And then there was Jock, her lifelong best friend. Sometimes afraid of her own shadow, often moody as hell and naive and boisterous when she wasn't, loyal, easy to confide in. They were so different; how could she be in love with both of them? And what was she to do with two lovers?

Maybe it wasn't love, she thought, opening the door to the student union building and stomping her feet to dislodge the snow from her boots. Maybe she was obsessed with sex. Or simply infatuated with the idea of being in love. After all, look at how quickly she had fallen in love with Blue; they had scarcely exchanged names and shared an orgasm when Jo had professed eternal love and adoration and the complete willingness to share her bed and her life forever. Poor Blue! No wonder she had seemed bemused. And no wonder she had withdrawn, kept something in reserve. It must have been quite unnerving to have an innocent one-night-stand swiftly turn into something more, something complicated.

If only she could have been decisive and ended their relationship when she had discovered that Blue had been unfaithful. On the other hand, what if she had been more understanding of Blue's need to feel unfettered, free? Would Blue have eventually grown tired of Suzanne? Jo would never know. She had been too jealous to think further than her own wounded ego, and she had turned to Jock for solace.

But Jock hadn't played fair. In the first place, she was always there, those big, blue eyes of hers filling their room with need. Who could have resisted? Certainly not Jo, whose feelings were already smarting from Blue's cavalier treatment. So Blue wanted a little independence? Well, then, so did Jo. But in retrospect, making love with Jock hadn't been a wise move, especially when she had discovered how good it felt and how strongly she was attracted to Jock. Who would have guessed? Stolid old Jock blowing her socks off in bed!

Jo took a tray and stood in line for a coffee, ignoring her dripping coat.

"Cutting classes again?"

She glanced sideways at Blue, who was busily loading down her tray with a tuna sandwich and a piece of chocolate cake. "No, they're finished for the day," she responded evenly, pouring coffee into a large, white mug. "Want one?"

"Sure."

Perhaps it was a good thing that they had met by chance, Jo thought; that way she wouldn't have to work up the nerve to call her.

"Over there," Blue said, gesturing with her tray to a table for two against one of the floor-to-ceiling glass windows.

"It's snowing again," Jo said unnecessarily, placing her damp coat over the back of the chair.

"What else is new?" Blue replied, sitting down and tearing the cellophane from her sandwich. "Want some sugar?"

Jo shook her head, deciding to take her coffee black, as if unadulterated caffeine would sharpen her wits and miraculously give her the ability to cope with Blue. And that was the problem, she mused as she sipped the strong, bitter coffee. She was always trying to cope with Blue, running to keep up only to find that when she finally got there Blue had moved on to another thought, another level, another woman, another world which more often than not Jo had never dreamed existed.

"So how have you been?" Blue asked, biting into her sandwich.

The smell of tuna assaulted Jo's nostrils. How could Blue eat at a time like this? It was so typical of her to act like she didn't care, to go on with ordinary things like eating and sleeping and studying when the world was falling apart around her. "I've been fine. Busy." But of course she'd been miserable. Confused. Unable to study.

"Good," Blue replied absently.

Blue's eating lunch was an act of obscenity, offending Jo and making her cross. She looked out the window at the falling snow and wondered how many centimetres they were going to get today. She hadn't listened to a weather forecast in weeks, so she was continually surprised when it snowed, and just as surprised when it didn't. What a winter. The misery of the weather was compounding the misery of her life. It was a good thing she didn't have to write a multiple choice exam on her emotional state, because she would fail abysmally.

"I've been spending a lot of time in the library," Blue volunteered, attacking her chocolate cake with gusto.

And I've been spending a lot of time staring into space, so it doesn't matter where I am, Jo thought angrily. Not that Blue cared; nobody could care and still eat like a damn pig. She resumed her snow watch, waiting for the wind to poke holes in the white blanket stretching in a straight line from sky to earth.

"Cat got your tongue?" Blue asked, pausing in her precise dissection of her piece of cake.

"Fuck off," Jo hissed, her face growing ruddy with anger.

Blue looked shocked, then chagrined, then amused. She dropped her fork on her plate, shoved the tray aside, placed her elbows on the table and looked at Jo. "Really?"

"No," Jo said; Blue deserved more than the proverbial finger and a wordless brush-off. "Not really."

"Good. You had me worried there for a moment," Blue said, a slight smile tempting the corners of her mouth.

"But we can't go on like this," Jo added, feeling like she was acting out the trite denouement in a trashy romance novel.

"It appeared to me as if we weren't going on at all," Blue responded.

Don't let her confuse you, Jo warned herself. "I think we should break up."

"Oh?" Blue's voice was soft, her expression unreadable.

"Officially."

"Oh."

Blue moved her tray back in front of her and calmly began polishing off the rest of her chocolate cake.

"Don't you even care?" Jo cried incredulously.

"Would it make any difference if I said I did?" Blue retorted, looking up at Jo for an instant, then directing her gaze back down to her plate and rather violently stabbing the large piece which remained.

Jo was taken aback. What did that mean? That Blue still loved her and didn't want to break up?

"Look, Jo, if you want to end our relationship, so be it. If you want it to continue with it, well, we can talk about that too. But make up your mind, will you? This indecision is driving me crazy," Blue said, carelessly tossing her fork on her plate. It landed with a clatter, but neither of them noticed.

"Are you saying that you want to be with me?" Jo dared to ask.

"I'm saying that I haven't ruled it out," Blue replied, "although I was fairly certain that you had."

Had she? What did she feel? It was true that she was tired of pretending to be more sophisticated than she was, of feeling ignorant in conversations on topics she knew nothing about, of laughing at jokes she didn't entirely understand, of hiding the wonder she felt each time she made love. This life was new to her; she couldn't see the city the way Blue did, as old, decaying and degenerate, a prime example of urban rot where everything had gone so wrong it was impossible for it to be put right again. While Blue tolerated urban life because she had to, Jo was fascinated by it. To Jo, Montreal was a bustling metropolis, a little down at the heels, to be sure, but full of history, new places to discover and interesting people to meet.

And more importantly, love was new to her. It was exciting, miraculous and fulfilling, and yet Blue philosophically questioned its very existence and distrusted its ability to make a difference in her life or anybody else's. Jo didn't ever want to feel like that. She didn't want sex to become utilitarian, something you did because it was part of human nature, like an unavoidable instinct or an itch which had to be scratched regularly. She wanted sex to retain its sense of mystery, its ability to take her out of herself, to transform everyday life. She never wanted to lose the sense of awe she felt when she was in the arms of her lover, and if that meant she was still immature, or a naive, small-town girl, then so what? Why should she change to keep up with somebody else, even her lover? Especially her lover.

"I think it would be better if we did break up," Jo replied slowly.

Blue nodded as if she had known her response all along. "Is it because of Jock?"

"No, it's because of me," Jo responded.

Blue nodded again and then, surprisingly, said, "Jock's not so bad."

Jo didn't reply; she could only think of one of them at a time, and

Jock's turn would undoubtedly come later. "Are you still seeing Suzanne?" she asked.

Blue didn't answer right away, so Jo knew that she was. But it didn't hurt so much any more, although she would always remember how she had felt that night when Blue had confessed. Everything had suddenly shifted, and the clarity of her beliefs had become muddied. "That's okay," she said softly.

"No it's not, but that's not your problem," Blue said with one of her charming smiles.

Jo didn't want to know more; Blue had started them on the unavoidable trail to decay, to the failure of their relationship. But what Blue did now, whether it was with Suzanne or with some other woman, was no longer her business. Perhaps she was a coward, but Jo didn't care to hear about it, and she certainly wasn't interested in why Blue had such an unhealthy fascination with Suzanne when she had admitted she didn't even like the woman. And the less she learned about sexual power tripping, the better.

"Jo, I want you to know that I really did care about you," Blue said with some difficulty, unable to meet her eyes for the first time that afternoon.

Well, now was certainly a fine time to be telling her. But Jo kept her temper in check and nodded, afraid that if she opened her mouth she would say something nasty.

"And I'm sorry I screwed up," Blue added.

That's awfully big of her, Jo thought sarcastically, and immediately felt sorry. "It doesn't matter."

"Now how did I know you were going to say that?" Blue said with a short laugh.

Because I'm so predictable. Because there's nothing else to say unless we open the floodgates and scream at each other. Because, because, because. Jo closed her eyes, suddenly tired. Was it always like this at the end, trite platitudes in lieu of — of what? Brutal honesty? Tears? Recrimination?

"Anyway, I've got to go," Blue said, rearranging the empty plates on her tray and then picking it up. "I'll see you around," she added.

"Sure."

"Maybe we can have coffee some time, or take in a movie," Blue suggested.

"Maybe," Jo replied, but she thought not; it was well and truly over.

"Maybe," Blue echoed somewhat sardonically. "Okay."
Go, Jo urged her with her mind. End this misery and go.

"Bye, then," Blue said, hovering, the dishes rattling as she attempted to balance the tray and carry her bulging briefcase at the same time.

"Bye."

Jo didn't say "see you around." And she didn't turn and watch Blue negotiate her way past the tightly packed tables or put her tray in the rack or slip from the cafeteria. She didn't have to; she could see her in her mind's eye, hear her leather coat crackling as she walked, recall the gracefulness with which she moved, imagine everything except the expression on her face. Was she sad? Relieved? Crying? Smiling? Thinking about her uncompleted thesis? On her way to call Suzanne? Deciding which bar to honour with her presence this evening? Planning a date with a new and previously unexplored possibility?

Jo shook her head to clear it but sadness clung to her like a residue of soot on the inside of a chimney which has just been cleaned. She lifted her coffee cup and sipped, not caring that it was cold; she felt too lethargic to get up for a refill.

She would soon go home and sleep it off, but for now, she was content to sit alone in the corner, to be bathed in the rhythmic flow of voices, to be soothed by the falling snow. And by the growing recognition that what had happened with Blue was right, that their futures were not intertwined, that somewhere out there she would find what she was looking for. As soon as she knew what it was.

# Soft Touch

"**I**'ve never slept in such a lumpy bed in all my life!" Oats complained emphatically, hopping dejectedly from one foot to the other in the open doorway of Melba's bedroom.

"Sue, for pete's sake, go to bed. I have to get up and go to work tomorrow morning," Melba retorted, shifting under the luxuriously thick woolbed she had inherited from her mother. Oats was envious. All she had was two nubby sheets which gravitated to her body during the night and wrapped themselves around her like an insecure lover, and a couple of ancient, scratchy wool blankets which smelled of dust and made her sneeze.

"But I can't sleep," Oats replied plaintively, slipping inside the room.

"Well go read a book, or watch TV or something," Melba said impatiently, switching to her side. "And close the door after you. Please."

Oats nervously checked the state of her heart and watched Melba twist and turn, wondering what she was thinking. Two weeks had passed, and nothing had changed. She was still a guest in Melba's house. She was desperately broke, dependant on Melba for breakfast, lunch and dinner. And if she could go out, she would probably have to ask for money to fill her gas tank. What a miserable state of affairs!

Having no money was bad enough, but Melba was still being nice to her. Oats didn't want kindness, to be on the receiving end of the type of smile you would politely bestow on some distant relative you had rescued from the poor house. Or worse, to be handled kindly like an old lover when you couldn't remember why on earth you ever loved her.

"Sue, go to bed!"

Sometimes she thought she would burst, that whole sentences would flow like vomit from her mouth, that all her unruly feelings would erupt like a volcano and suddenly Melba would be over-whelmed and the wall would come tumbling down, like it had in Berlin. Except Oats didn't know if she had that kind of power left in her.

"What are you doing out there?" Melba demanded, her patience at an end. She sat up and switched on her bedside table lamp, her face flushed, her hair dishevelled. She looked beautiful, Oats thought. Stunning.

"Sue, answer me!"

"Looking at you," Oats said, her voice gruff. "You look great."

"Well I won't look so great in the morning if I don't get some sleep," Melba snapped, reaching to turn out the light. "Now go away and leave me in peace."

But the problem was that Oats couldn't find any of that elusive peace lying there alone on that narrow, lumpy sofa-bed in the next room, listening to the rhythmic drip of the bathroom tap as Melba slept, waiting against hope for her door to open, for the sound of bare feet slapping on the varnished wood floor, for the weight of an additional body to stretch the springs of the narrow sofa-bed, for warm lips and hands to reach out and touch her. Because no matter how long and patiently she waited or how much she hoped, Melba never came.

"Sue!"

Oats smiled through her terror and slid under the covers, pulling Melba's woolbed up under her chin, trying to ignore how fast her heart was beating. Don't give out on me now, she warned it. She wasn't finished living yet, not by a long shot. And she deserved some reward for being good; no cigarettes, although she had almost died from longing the first time she smelled smoke, no booze, no fried or fatty foods. Not that Melba would ever let a fried chicken cross her threshold and spread its grease on one of her plates, oh no; the diet she was on would make even the strictest nutritionist seem unhealthy by comparison. Melba would probably throw the offending plate in the garbage if cholesterol so much as touched it. Oats felt like a damn chipmunk from all those lettuce leaves and grains and tofu and nuts and bolts and whatever, and the problem was, they all tasted like cardboard. Except when they tasted like grass. Big difference. No wonder she was always hungry. No wonder her body craved nicotine. No wonder she pined for a beer. No wonder she was so horny that she felt like she was going to explode.

"Just what do you think you're doing?" Melba demanded hotly, sitting up again.

"Getting warm," Oats replied calmly, saved by the knowledge that it was partially true. Those uncovered wood floors were cold on the feet in the middle of the night when the heat was turned down to near zero.

"Go get warm in your own bed," Melba retorted coldly.

"Melba," Oats pleaded, reaching out her hand and grasping Melba's shoulder.

"Sue, don't."

"I have to," Oats mumbled. "Somebody has to, and if it's not going to be you, then it has to be me."

"What a load of garbage," Melba scoffed. "Now come to your senses and go to bed."

How could she be so stubborn? What was it going to take, dynamite? "No," Oats replied with a calmness she didn't feel. She placed a reassuring hand over her heart, but her heart was so busy doing its own thing that it didn't respond to her touch. She could feel it thumping rapidly in her chest, and a lump of fear grew in her throat. Was she going to die right here and now, before she could make Melba listen to her?

"Sue, be reasonable," Melba said. "Go back to bed and let me get some sleep. You don't belong here any more."

There it was, that horrible kindness again. "Oh yes I do," Oats retorted, raising herself on an elbow and forgetting about her heart. "Oh yes I do."

"Damn you!"

Oats' wildly nervous heart slowed and her muscles relaxed and then grew strong with another kind of tension as she felt Melba's fingers touch her cheek and softly run across her lips. She opened her mouth and gently licked the tips of her fingers, then drew them in. After more a month of abstinence, this simple intimacy was like an orgasm and Oats immediately grew aroused, wet.

"Oh, Sue. You fool."

But Oats knew better. It was right, it was the next step, the only step. She pulled Melba to her and they kissed chastely, mouths closed, savouring their growing passion. Oats opened her mouth and unbuttoned Melba's nightgown, growing breathless as she touched Melba, stroking the familiar flesh which had been available to her only in her dreams. She felt Melba's hands move rapidly over her body, and her skin rippled.

"You've grown thin," Melba whispered in her ear.

"Yeah, ain't that a laugh," Oats whispered back.

"I feel like I'm in bed with a different woman," Melba added, cupping Oats' breasts.

"Don't make me jealous," Oats said lightly, returning the gesture.

Melba laughed, but her hands stilled.

"I'm just kidding," Oats said reassuringly, running her hands down over Melba's belly and into the wet warmth between her legs. She stroked Melba, feeling her hips begin to circle as the wetness grew. She had been right to make the first move a sexual one; making love would re-establish their intimacy and make it easier to talk later.

"Does this feel good?" Melba asked, stroking rhythmically.

"Hmmm," Oats responded appreciatively, but she was worried; she didn't like the rush of blood to her head or the strong sound of her heartbeat reverberating in her ears. She took a deep breath and slowed down.

"What wrong?"

"I don't know," she replied nervously.

"Should I be doing something different?" Melba asked.

"No, no. That feels good," Oats reassured her.

"Well then, what?"

"It's just my heart," Oats whispered miserably.

"Are you in pain?" Melba said at once, her body immediately growing tense.

"No. But it's beating too fast," Oats said, her hands still.

"Oh, Sue. Your heart always beats faster when you're excited. Everyone's does," Melba said, planting an affectionate kiss on her forehead.

"Are you sure?" Oats asked, feeling dubious. After all, Melba wasn't the one who had nearly died. And to tell the truth, Oats had never paid much attention to her heart. It had always been there, ticking away the seconds, minutes, hours, days, weeks, months, years, decades. She had taken it for granted, as something mother nature put there, like your big toe or your underarm hair or some horrid-looking internal organ which was thankfully tucked out of sight. Nobody ever questioned why they had this big toe or asked themselves what would happen if it suddenly dropped off without any warning whatsoever. Still, if one day when you were running barefoot in the sand you noticed that you had left your big toe behind, wouldn't it be natural to start wondering when the other one was going to play the same trick on you, that some fateful night when you took off your sneakers, your last remaining big toe would have unilaterally decided that it preferred to inhabit your running shoe rather than face another long day of pounding the pavement and scaling the endless steps from the subway? Well, that was precisely how Oats felt about her heart. She couldn't depend on it any more, because it was just as likely to go off half-cocked as one of those archetypal big toes and leave her in the lurch at a crucial moment. Except that losing a big toe wasn't the same as losing your life.

"Making love isn't going to cause another heart attack," Melba assured her.

"I don't know!" Oats cried, frustrated. But wait a minute. Moderate exercise. They said she could partake in some regular, moderate exercise. In fact, they had even strongly suggested she do just that very thing. But she hadn't thought to ask whether sex was included in their definition of moderate exercise, and of course they hadn't volunteered that particular information. They probably thought that since she was a single woman, it didn't matter anyway. Or maybe they never mentioned it to anybody. What? Sex? Why do you want to know about that? Hey, be grateful that you're still alive!

"Do you want to stop?" Melba asked softly.

"No. Yes. *No!*" Oats replied, shifting her hand, which had grown cramped between Melba's thighs, then moving her fingers back and forth over that soft, lovely flesh.

"Are you sure?"

"Yes," Oats replied emphatically. Was Melba nuts? Of course she wasn't sure. But she would rather die than lose sex from her life. Big toes she could do without; sex she couldn't. How to procure an orgasm for herself had been her biggest problem during the two weeks she had spent in the hospital; it had been ridiculously difficult to get her arm down under the sheets and between her legs with all those nasty needles sticking out the back of her hand. And once her fingers had reached their target, she had been forced to concentrate on keeping her mouth shut and her hips still, which wasn't easy when you were the type to wail and throw yourself about with great abandon. Then of course she had worried whether diddling herself would send her heart monitor into a frenzy, resulting in a flock of nurses descending on her and discovering her in *flagrante delicto*, so to speak. But it had never happened, because she had never orgasmed. Maybe she had been too worried about being found out;

after all, there was no privacy, and masturbating in the hospital was like trying to do it in the top bunk in a crowded cabin at camp with only the whispering murmur of the waves on the nearby lake and the irregular snores of other little girls as quite insufficient cover. Or perhaps she hadn't had enough energy. Or will power. Or maybe she was never going to come again. There was always that, of course, unthinkable as it was. "Yeah, I'm sure," she repeated, this time with grim determination. "Don't stop."

Oats felt Melba's smile spread on her cheek, a smile which widened as Melba took her on a long sensual trip with mountain peaks interspersed with the inevitable valleys. Whispers grew more urgent, sounds turned to symbols until the symbols themselves became meaningless and only pleasure remained, the pleasure of reconciliation, of shared passion, of the touch of skin on skin, of the final release which, when it came, left Oats bathed in sweat, her heart still intact. Emotionally exhausted, sexually sated, arms and legs wrapped possessively around Melba, she slept.

"Rise and shine!"

Oats reached for Melba, and although the sheets beside her were warm, no one was there. She groaned and turned over, snuggling deeper into the marvellous woolbed. It felt far too early to wake up.

"Breakfast is ready!"

She could smell coffee. Her eyes opened and met Melba's.

"Good morning," Melba whispered, kissing her gently.

"Huh." Oats hated people who were cheerful in the morning, although she swiftly resolved to never again hold it against Melba, not after last night.

"I see that hasn't changed," Melba said, sounding amused.

"Come back to bed, woman, and I'll show you what hasn't changed," Oats threatened, throwing off the woolbed to expose her naked body, then stretching tantalizingly.

"Don't tempt me, Sue. I can't possibly be late for work this morning, I've got a meeting first thing," Melba replied, looking away.

"Oh." Disappointed and chilly, Oats covered herself; except for late in the afternoon, when the landlord begrudged them a short blast of heat, it was always cold in Melba's apartment.

"Come on, I've made breakfast," Melba said, slipping into her suit jacket and leaving the bedroom.

But she liked sex in the morning, Oats grumbled to herself, getting out of bed and retrieving her pajamas from the floor. Furthermore, now that she knew she was still capable of orgasming with the best of them, she was eager to make up for lost time. Just think of all those missed opportunities, the weeks she had spent chastely waiting for Melba to return, not to mention the forced abstinence she had suffered in the hospital. She deserved a day in bed with her lover!

"What's this?" Oats asked, trudging into the kitchen and peering suspiciously into her half-filled bowl.

"You know very well what it is," Melba said with an amused smile. "You've had it every day for the past two weeks."

"Of course I know, but that isn't the point," Oats explained patiently, sitting down and shoving her spoon into the obnoxious mixture of seeds, chopped nuts, grains and dried fruit. "The point is that I don't like it," she said stridently, shoving a spoonful of that absurd excuse for a breakfast into her mouth.

"Put some milk on it, then," Melba suggested.

"I don't like milk, either," Oats grumbled.

"You don't like anything that's good for you, do you?" Melba calmly stated.

"Well, I wouldn't go so far as to say that," Oats replied between mouthfuls.

"Name me one thing you like that's good for you, then," Melba said challengingly.

"Sex," Oats replied immediately.

"You know what I mean, you dolt!"

"You mean you think that sex isn't good for me?" Oats demanded mockingly.

"Oh, you're impossible. Shut up and eat your cereal," Melba retorted.

Oats smiled victoriously, and graciously consented to consume another mouthful. "Are we going to live here forever or are you coming home with me?" she asked once she had finished chewing and swallowing the damn stuff, a laborious task if there ever was one.

Melba didn't reply.

Oh oh, Oats thought worriedly, watching conflicting emotions compete for space on Melba face. She put down her spoon and rested her elbows on the table. Now she had done it; she had spoken too soon, and ended up with her foot in her mouth, which obviously wasn't going to taste any better than Melba's breakfast concoction.

"Why don't we talk about that later? When we have a little more time," Melba responded, glancing at the wall clock.

"Okay," Oats replied, relieved that she was off the hook, at least temporarily.

Melba studied her face. Oats willed it to be expressionless. The last thing she wanted was for the spell of last night's intimacy to be broken.

"Really?"

"Yes," Oats said.

"Good."

Oats watched Melba rise from her chair and carry her dishes to the counter, and suddenly she realized that she hadn't lied, that it really was okay. After all, she had nearly died without having the opportunity to make amends and to seriously try to make her relationship with Melba work, and now she had a second and basically undeserved second chance.

It was like crying in the hospital; at first she hadn't remembered how to cry, then she hadn't known what to cry about, and finally she had cried about every last little thing. Well, being honest, being faithful, being *there* for Melba was something like that, Oats mused as Melba bent down and kissed her. She had hardly any experience in being honest, even less in being faithful, and none at all in actually being there through thick and thin, through hell and high water, through sickness and in health. Wasn't that how it went? Maybe it wasn't so meaningless after all.

She was new to honesty, a novice when it came to faithfulness. She would have to learn how to care. Poor Melba. Poor, poor Melba. She was stuck with a different type of virgin. Oats only hoped that Melba would decide it was worth it.

# Four O'clock and
# All's Well

What was it that Blue had said? That she and Jo were a natural? If she hadn't quaffed so many beers, she would undoubtedly be able to remember Blue's exact words. She had downed three at the bar, and then she and Blue had gone back to Blue's apartment and finished off a case of twelve. Jock had fallen into a uneasy, inebriated sleep on the sofa in Blue's living room and nearly had to crawl home on her hands and knees the next morning, suffering from one of the worst hangovers of her life. Even the dingy snow had been bright enough to make her want to throw up, not to mention how the speeding, rolling bus had made her gorge rise and nearly overflow.

What a strange apartment Blue had. Imagine living with black walls. Except for her bedroom, which had been painted bright red, even the ceiling. Blue sure wouldn't be able to make a living as interior decorator, she thought with a snicker.

No, but what had Blue meant by that remark? A natural what? Jock flung her chemistry book across the room, not caring that the cover popped off when it landed on her bed and then bounced to the floor.

Damn Blue anyway for putting ideas in her mind. Not that Jock hadn't had them before, but she didn't need encouragement. Why was she suffering from this stupid unrequited love for Jo when she could probably have her choice of any one of a number of women? Not Candy, though. No, never again with Candy. That had been a colossal mistake from start to finish. Candy had changed from a hard-nosed pool player with a sense of humour into a blathering drunk. Jock had ignored it at first, desperate to get her to bed and superimpose sex with somebody else over her vivid memories of making love with Jo. Of course it hadn't worked, she had been silly to think that it would. And Candy drunk was no prize; after so many drinks that Jock was at a loss to explain why she was still conscious, Candy had rambled through several sordid stories which didn't make the least bit of sense, whispered secrets which were unbelievably boring, and in general went through so many mood swings that Jock felt like she was conversing with a yo-yo. Mind you, once Candy got to bed and shut up, the sex had been great. Still, there were lots of other women in the world, so why wasn't she out there getting some? Had she been born stupid, or had she just grown into it?

She sighed, got up, and retrieved her chemistry text, balancing it in the palm of her hand. It fell off again, leaving her holding the empty cover. It was certainly lighter that way. And there was sure a lot less to learn, she thought with another snicker. Aw, why should she even bother? She was going to fail the exam anyway. She kicked the coverless textbook under the desk and fell on her bed, dropping the cover beside her. Maybe she should go down the hall and see if Tony had any beer. But Tony had taken to drinking rum and coke, which Jock didn't particularly like; it make her drunk so fast that she didn't have time to enjoy getting there. Still, Tony was right; it was much easier to smuggle a bottle of rum into the dorm than a case of beer, and you could always buy coke in the vending machine in the basement.

"Studying hard, I see," Jo commented, closing the door behind her.

"You bet," Jock replied, holding up the cover of her chemistry textbook.

"I thought you had an exam tomorrow," Jo said, opening the closet door and hanging her coat on the first available hanger.

"Don't remind me," Jock said with a false shiver.

"It's nearly ten. Don't you think you should get to it?"

Jock watched Jo sit on her bed, open her briefcase and remove a thick library book, which she immediately started to read. At least Jo was talking to her now. The silent treatment was over, not that Jock understood why. But then, she hadn't been able to decide what had started it in the first place. It couldn't have been because of Candy, could it? And what had Blue said?

"What are you sighing about now?" Jo asked abruptly, closing her book with a thump.

"Don't pick on me," Jock muttered, not feeling particularly charitable.

"Me pick on *you*," Jo exclaimed, rising from her bed. "I come home and the room is a mess, you haven't bothered to change your clothes in days, and to top it all off, you're in a despicable mood!"

"A des-pic-a-ble mood," Jock repeated, mimicking Jo in a singsong voice. "A des-pic-a-ble mood," she chanted again, sitting up and flinging the empty book cover across the room. It hit the wall over Jo's bed and slid to the floor. "You bet I'm in a des-pic-a-ble mood," she said emphatically, getting up. "And do you want to know why?"

"Why?" Jo whispered, her eyes wide like those of a startled dear frozen in place by the headlights of an oncoming car.

"Because I'm in love with you," Jock said, turning away. "I'm in love with you, damn it. That's all."

Devastated by what she had said, she fell face first on her bed, covering her head with her pillow. There was nothing for it; she was a fool, a pure and simple fool.

"Oh Jock. You idiot."

That too, Jock thought. That too. Tell me more, I'm just a glutton for punishment these days.

"Come on, Jock," Jo cajoled. Jock felt her sit on the bed and try to remove the pillow from her head. She held on for dear life, certain that she would disappear in a whiff of smoke or self-destruct into a zillion pieces if Jo saw her face.

"Jock, stop being so silly," Jo said.

Jo was laughing at her; she could hear it in her voice. "I'll be silly any time I want to," Jock replied, her voice muffled by the dusty pillow.

"Can I join you, then?" Jo whispered, and suddenly Jock felt Jo straddle her. "Let me in."

Her hands tightened on the pillow, but to no avail; Jo's weight was smothering her, and before she knew it, a second head was forcing itself under the pillow.

"Hi, there," Jo said casually.

Just what did she think she was doing? Didn't she have any respect?

"Phew! Don't you ever change your pillowcase?" Jo complained, sneezing.

"And didn't your mother teach you to cover your nose and mouth when you sneeze?" Jock shot back.

"Give me a kiss," Jo said with a giggle, snuggling closer until their noses were touching.

"No!" Jock said, stubbornly holding out even though her body was tingling.

"Don't be so mean," Jo complained, and then she pulled off the pillow and kissed her.

Hadn't Jo heard what she said? And what about Blue? "Stop," Jock said, her hands moving to prevent Jo from opening her shirt.

"Why?" Jo pushed her hands away and tugged her shirt from her jeans, spreading it, exposing Jock's breasts. Her nipples were already hard, as if they had already guessed Jo's next move, which was to swoop down and suck them into her mouth, one after another. Jock shivered.

"Do you really want me to stop?" Jo whispered, pausing to look up at Jock, smiling when she saw the expression on Jock's face, then getting back to serious work.

"I'm so confused," Jock confessed. And her confusion was growing in tandem with her arousal as Jo unzipped her jeans and slid them down over her hips.

"Love can do that to you," Jo replied, slipping her hand between Jock's thighs.

Jock moaned.

"That's good," Jo whispered.

"But I love you," Jock said mournfully.

"That's even better," Jo replied.

"But do you — do you — "

"Shhh. Feel this."

Oh, Jock felt it all right, all the way home. She orgasmed swiftly, clutching Jo to her, never wanting to let go, never wanting her to stop.

"Good," Jo said in a self-satisfied voice. She disentangled herself from Jock and stood up to get undressed. Jock watched as her sweater and jeans fell to the floor, swiftly followed by her bra and panties. She is so beautiful, Jock thought. So gorgeous. How could she not be out of reach?

"Do you love me?" Jock blurted as Jo laid down beside her.

Jo pulled a blanket over them and then rose on her elbow, looking down at Jock.

Oh no, Jock thought, panicking. It was going to be bad, really bad. She had confessed her love and opened herself to total destruction. How could Jo possibly love her? She was nothing, less than nothing. A stupid, bumbling hick from small-town Quebec. A dumb bunny who couldn't even pass one single exam. An uncoordinated dolt who wasn't good enough to make the basketball team. An inexperienced lover who was never sure what to do next, who was certain that she was either going too fast or not fast enough. She couldn't compete with women like Blue even if she tried.

"You don't love me," she mumbled, turning her head away, wishing she could slip down the crack between the bed and the wall.

"I didn't say that," Jo said, reaching out and stroking her cheek.

"You didn't have to," Jock replied, fatally wounded. Could you die of heartache?

"Jock, don't try to read my mind, because you can't," Jo warned, smiling to take the sting from her words.

"But — "

"Stop talking and listen for a minute," Jo interrupted, dropping from her elbow and cuddling against Jock's neck. Jock put her arms around her and said nothing.

"This has been a crazy year for both of us," Jo said, stating the obvious.

"You're not kidding," Jock replied with evident feeling.

"And going away to college wasn't all it was supposed to be," Jo added.

"Tell me about it," Jock whispered.

"Everything went wrong for you, didn't it?"

Jock nodded, feeling close to tears. She hugged Jo tighter, taking comfort in her closeness.

"You couldn't settle down and study, so you aren't doing so well in your courses," Jo said.

What an understatement! She was going to fail, and fail abysmally. How was she going to tell her parents? What could she say? Sorry folks, I spent your money goofing off and trying to get laid, and then I flunked out?

"You didn't make the basketball team, either," Jo added.

"Neither did you," Jock reminded her.

"But I didn't really care, not the way you did," Jo said. "You really wanted to play. I just went along for the ride, and if I made the team fine, if not, well, that was fine too. I had enough of that stuff in high school. I wanted to do different things here."

Different things. Like going out to the bars instead of sweating her way up and down the basketball court, Jock thought. Like meeting lots of women instead of sitting for hours on the team bus, bored stiff but unable to read because she got motion sickness whenever she tried. Like scoring in a whole new way by finding a lover and making love on a regular basis rather than tossing a ball through a hoop, which, when you thought about it, was a pretty meaningless way to pass the time.

"And there you were, depressed because you didn't make the team and you were failing your courses, and then you fell in love with me."

Jo had known the whole time. Jock felt like an ignoramus; had she been that obvious?

"Yeah, well — "

"Shhh. I'm not finished yet," Jo scolded, giving her a kiss on the forehead. "And what about me? Do you think I've had it easy all this time?" Jo asked.

"I don't know," Jock admitted.

"You might have been in love with me, but you weren't really paying attention to what I was going through," Jo said.

"Now wait a minute — "

"Don't go all defensive on me, Jock. That's not why I'm telling you this."

"Oh."

Jo shifted, moving back so she could look at Jock's face. "We were both part of a pretty tight group back there in high school, and it wasn't easy for me to lose that support, either. And no matter how much we wanted to go, it's hard to leave home. Suddenly there's nobody there to keep tabs on you, or tell you what to do. When you get in trouble, you have to work it out for yourself."

And of course she hadn't capable of working her way out of a paper bag, Jock thought, while Jo had. She sighed; did Jo really think that this was going to make her feel better about herself?

"And then I fell in love with Blue," Jo continued.

Jock willed her to just shut up, go away and leave her alone with her misery.

But she didn't. "And for awhile it was great. I was really in love with her, you know."

Jock forced herself to nod.

"And then Blue got involved with Suzanne."

"You don't have to talk about it," Jock reassured her, hoping that she would take the hint.

"No, you have to know," Jo told her.

Oh no she didn't. But she didn't say anything; she was afraid that Jo would think she didn't care.

"When I first found out, I was devastated. You see, I never had anything like that happen to me before. I always got whatever I wanted, but with Blue, for the first time in my life I couldn't control what was happening. I could rant and rave or cry or beg, but I couldn't stop Blue from going her own way."

"Mmm."

"But you knew that all along, didn't you?"

Jock grew alert. "What?"

"You realized that people do what they want to no matter how much you want them to do something different. You knew that it wasn't any use to try to make people over. And that being in love doesn't solve all your problems," Jo answered.

"Sometimes it creates more problems than it solves," Jock responded dryly, thinking of how she felt about Jo.

"Exactly. But you see, I didn't know this. I thought that all I had to do was fall in love and things would automatically fall into place," Jo said. "Dumb, huh?"

What, was Jo calling herself dumb? Why, she was the smartest woman Jock knew. Didn't she know that? Couldn't she see how wonderful she was?

"Yeah, dumb," Jo answered herself. "I stupidly tried to make Blue into my dream woman."

"Your dream woman?" Jock said, involuntarily giggling.

Jo blushed. "You know, the woman you imagine is going to love you like crazy and give you everything you need for the rest of your life."

"Oh. That one," Jock snickered self-consciously. Well, of course she had one of those; didn't everybody? But how had Jo ever imagined that Blue was her "dream woman"? A skinny punk with spikes for hair? An anarchist in a leather jacket? A jaded bar dyke aiming for her PhD in some arcane topic Jock had never managed to fully understand, mainly because she never listened when Blue was talking about it? She was beginning to think that Jo had been born yesterday, which somehow reassured her.

"Blue was the first woman I fell in love with, and I guess I put too much pressure on her," Jo added. "And she reacted by getting involved with someone else. I understand that now."

"Mmm." Jock pulled the blanket up around her shoulders and then tucked it around Jo, rubbing her back in passing.

"That feels good," Jo told her, nuzzling her neck.

Jock planted little kisses all over Jo's face, feeling shy even though Jo's eyes were closed.

"Kiss me," Jo whispered.

There. And there. And again.

"That's so nice," Jo purred. "Where was I?" she asked, her voice husky. "You got me all distracted."

"Blue," Jock replied glumly, falling back with a sigh.

"Yes, well, I broke up with her," Jo said.

Jock turned over, rocking the mattress. The sagging bedsprings creaked protestingly. "You did?"

Jo nodded. "I guess I still care about her, but it's not the same."

"Why not?" Jock asked, daring to hope. Not much, and maybe even that was unfounded, but she couldn't help herself. For such a consistent loser, she was incorrigibly optimistic.

"Because of you, silly," Jo replied with an affectionate grin. "Why else?"

Naw. It couldn't be. She had fallen asleep and started to dream. "Pinch me," she said.

Jo laughed.

Jock cut her off with an enthusiastic kiss. "Oh, I love you so much."

"And I love you too," Jo responded, suddenly serious.

It was the most important moment of Jock's life. "You do?"

Jo nodded. "But you'll have to be patient with me, Jock. There are still some things I have to work out."

But Jock didn't want to know about patience, not now, not when she had the whole world in her hands. She reached under the covers and cupped Jo's breasts, feeling her nipples harden. These lovely, full breasts were hers. This body too was hers, to touch, to adore, to love. And this woman, this friend she had wanted for as long as she could remember, since desire had first stirred in her teenage soul, was hers. All hers. Passion flared and she moved her hand lower, cupping Jo's crotch, staring into Jo's eyes, letting Jo see what she was feeling.

"Come here, you," Jo commanded softly, and Jock went. Immediately and willingly.

But all things come to an end, even extravagant ones involving two young women in the throes of passion, and by four o'clock in the morning, both of them were sated. Temporarily, for sure, but it was all too evident in the languid sprawl of their tangled bodies, in the sweat-matted sweep of their dishevelled hair, in the sleepy blankness peeping through their half-closed eyes.

Jo stirred and gave Jock a slap on the rear.

Jock jumped, startled. "What?"

"Hit the books, lover," Jo responded.

"Now? Are you nuts? It's four in the morning!"

"If you think I'm going to let you flunk out and leave me to the mercy of a new roommate, you're crazy," Jo said emphatically, sitting up and giving Jock another slap on the behind.

"Oh, no," Jock moaned.

"And with my luck, I'll end up with some unspeakably gorgeous creature on the prowl," Jo continued, ignoring Jock's protests.

"Oh, no," Jock moaned, louder this time.

"With boobs the size of watermelons," Jo added.

"I can't believe you," Jock wailed plaintively, sitting up.

"A real sex maniac," Jo teased.

"Where's my chemistry book?" Jock muttered, falling to the floor and crawling under the desk to retrieve the coverless textbook.

"What a view!" Jo exclaimed.

"Oh, shut up," Jock muttered, although she wasn't too embarrassed to wriggle her bum in what she hoped was a suitably provocative manner.

"Put something on before I ravish you," Jo told her.

"I wish," Jock said fervently, backing out from under the desk.

"Anything but chemistry, right?"

"Right."

"I don't know if that's much of a compliment, but I'll take it anyway," Jo said with a laugh.

Jock went to the closet and took out her housecoat, slipping it on. She settled herself at the desk, opening the discouragingly thick book. How many pages had they covered? And how much did she remember? She flipped through several chapters, sighed and then turned back to page one; the only thing to do was start at the beginning and cover as many chapters as she could. It was a good thing the exam wasn't until two in the afternoon. Seven or eight hours of cramming would at least give her a fighting chance.

"Shall I get you a coffee?" Jo asked.

"Maybe later," Jock replied absently, her mind busily digesting formulae, building a base for the more complex equations which would undoubtedly follow.

"I'll keep you company and read my book in bed," Jo said, carrying Jock's pillow to her bed and placing it on top of her own.

"You don't have to," Jock assured her. "I'm okay."

"I know. But I want to," Jo said with a smile.

Jock turned to page two of her book, surprisingly touched. Jo cared about her. Hey, maybe this love stuff really had something going for it. And maybe it hadn't been such a bad year after all.

# Indecision

Blue left the telephone booth and plodded through the snow. "Come on over," Suzanne had said in that deep, sexy voice of hers. Come and get it was what she had meant. Come play with me. Come get laid. Come have your ego stripped, your limits challenged, your soul scalded, all in the name of good sex. But by whose definition, Blue wondered?

She kicked the snow, suddenly feeling desolate. She was emotionally empty, and not the least bit horny. She had been feeling increasingly asexual ever since Jo broke up with her. And what she did with Suzanne was making things worse instead of better. Everything both fascinated and repulsed her: the dominance, the increaingly blatant violence, her ex-lover Karen's newly discovered voyeurism. Suzanne was opening doors Blue would have preferred to leave closed, even locked. Although it was supposed to be nothing more than casual sex, with a good time had by all, over the months their affair had taken an obsessive hold on her. Her ambivalence weakened when they were together, then grew strong when they were apart. Her relationship with Jo hadn't mattered when Suzanne was playing with Blue's body and toying with her mind, but when she had been with Jo, she had felt guilty. And relieved. Compared to Suzanne, Jo was a marvel of simplicity: truthful, loving and honest in bed, while Suzanne, well, Suzanne was Suzanne. Dishonesty aroused her. Defining the fine line between sex and violence excited her. She was ruthless, fearlessly taking Blue to the edge, then over. But never too far. Blue was constantly on the verge of saying "no," but Suzanne knew precisely when to pull back or to push a different button. The resulting ecstasy always silenced Blue's refusal before it left her lips.

Suzanne destroyed her ability to resist oppression by inner forces she hated and wanted to overcome, forces which she had always refused to recognize. Suzanne smiled a certain way and Blue melted. Suzanne snapped her fingers and Blue went running. Suzanne touched her and Blue shivered with uncontrollable passion. Suzanne abused her and Blue had an orgasm. No wonder she was depressed. Before this madness with Suzanne, Blue had always been ethical in her relationships. She hadn't lied; she hadn't said she loved someone when it wasn't true. She hadn't cheated, even when the opportunity arose. And she hadn't betrayed the values she had believed in. Still did believe in.

"Come on over."

But she didn't want to go. She wanted to forget every sexual act she had ever performed with Suzanne. She wanted to turn back the clock to a more innocent time, to a time when she hadn't spent all her waking moments feeling guilty. To when she had been content to dabble with the idea of letting herself fall in love with Jo. But that was over. Jo was with Jock, and here she was, being drawn once again to Suzanne, like a moth to a lightbulb, to a night of trickery, where nothing was what it seemed to be. Why couldn't she accept that there were some unmapped, subterranean pathways it was better to leave unexplored?

Jo had been crushed. Devastated. And it had been all Blue's fault. How could she be so obsessed with meaningless sex? With sex which shamed her? Because it was so exciting, a little voice answered. Because it was like nothing she had ever experienced before. Because she felt strong, perverse excitement when she was out of control, when the only thing between her and sexual abyss was Suzanne's firm hand, Suzanne's strength, Suzanne's unstated promise that she wouldn't hurt Blue or let Blue hurt herself.

"Come on over."

No. I won't go. Not tonight, at least, Blue vowed. And I won't call, either. Let her wonder for a change. But she felt too lonely to go back to her apartment. And anyway, it stank of cheap paint. She could always go home and paint the rest of the night away, brush on that third coat of white paint which would finally succeed in covering the black. Next week she would do her bedroom; red was an inappropriate colour for a woman who barely had any sexual feelings left, whose sex drive was almost gone.

She turned around and went to the bar.

"Well, well. Look what the cat dragged in," Candy said, dropping her pool cue on the table.

"Hi, stranger," Blue replied, smiling, tossing her jacket into a corner.

"Buy me a beer?"

Blue nodded and followed Candy to the bar.

"This place is as boring as a cemetery tonight," Candy complained.

"What? No date?" Blue teased.

"You should talk," Candy retorted.

Blue laughed. "How about a game?"

"You got it," Candy agreed.

They walked back to the deserted pool table and Candy racked the balls.

"Do you know that little jerk had the nerve to walk out on me?" Candy said as she began shooting.

"Who, Jock?"

"Who else?"

"Oh, well. There's always more fish in the sea," Blue said lightly.

"She said I drank too much," Candy added, finally missing a shot.

"Well, you do, don't you?" Blue commented.

"Why shouldn't I?"

"Why should you?"

"You're up," Candy said, stepping away from the table. "Life's such a drag," she added casually, picking up her beer and finishing it.

"There is that," Blue agreed, taking a sip from her beer bottle before setting it down. Her mind wasn't on pool, and she missed her first shot.

"Hey, you can do better than that," Candy complained.

"My mind isn't on the game," Blue admitted.

"No kidding! Well, do you want to go back to my place and have sex?" Candy asked, sinking a couple of shots before she paused and looked up at Blue.

"Not really," Blue replied.

"Oh, come on. Neither of us have got anything better to do," she cajoled.

Blue communicated her disinterest with a shrug. She wasn't into having sex simply because she was at loose ends. Or bored. Besides, she had no intention of getting involved with Candy again. She really was drinking too much, and Blue didn't want to be a spectator, or, even worse, an active participant when Candy's life came crashing down around her. Anyway, the kind of casual sex Candy preferred no longer had any attraction for Blue.

"Jeez, you're in some kind of mood!" Candy complained. "Well, want to get high instead?"

"On what?" Blue asked, curious.

"Whatever you like," Candy replied, sinking another couple of balls. "I've got some stuff at home, and I can get something different if you don't like that."

"I think I'll pass," Blue said.

Candy threw her pool cue to the floor, where it clattered against the brick wall. "What's the matter with you, anyway? Too good for somebody like me now that you're nearly a doctor of something or other?" she asked bitterly.

"Have another beer and calm down," Blue said in a mild voice, refusing to be baited. She went to the bar and bought two more beers, giving one to Candy. It's nothing personal, she thought. Candy's just upset because she doesn't have a lover tonight. And I'm upset because I have a lover I don't want but can't stay away from.

She laughed at herself and said, "okay, let's really play this time. A buck a shot."

"You're on," Candy replied instantly. "I can beat you with one hand tied behind my back."

"Just try it," Blue retorted.

"Watch me," Candy leered.

The night passed. Beer bottles were emptied and tossed under the table. Money exchanged hands. And when the bar closed, Blue did what she said she wouldn't even though she was still sober; she drove Candy home, smoked some dope with her, and then got into bed and made love to her. It doesn't mean a thing, she told herself as she laboured over Candy. Tomorrow is another day and that doesn't mean a thing either. Maybe tomorrow I'll shave my head. Maybe the day after I'll flush my thesis down the toilet and drop out of school. Maybe I'll stay stoned for the rest of my life. Maybe Suzanne will beg me to come back. Or to stay away. Maybe Candy will forget this ever happened. Maybe I'll move away and never return. She felt Candy reach up and pull her closer, and then she came, but that didn't mean anything either. She felt nothing. It was like her body was dead and her clit anaesthetized, its connection to reality severed. Stoned and depressed, she fell asleep.

"Let's have breakfast out," Candy said, waking her with an elbow in the ribs.

"Let's take a shower first," Blue suggested, turning over, her nose twitching. Their bodies smelled of stale cigarette smoke, spilled beer, night-long, low-down sex. It was rather disgusting, although perhaps that was simply her state of mind, since she had never been adverse to wallowing in sex before.

"Let's take one together," Candy replied. "Do you want a beer?"

"No, it's too early. And you shouldn't either," Blue answered.

"Get off my back," Candy retorted.

"So do what you want," Blue said with a shrug. "It's your life, after all."

"You're damn right," Candy said bitterly.

Blue went into the bathroom and ran the shower, not waiting for Candy to come back. She stepped into the water and washed herself, then let the spray pummel her back. It felt good. She was about to turn off the shower when Candy joined her, beer bottle in hand. Don't make judgements when you don't know anything about the limits of somebody else's pain or their ability to tolerate it, Blue told herself. Candy is who she is. She can't help it, and she obviously isn't capable of changing. Not right now, anyway. Suzanne is who she is. And I am who I am. Jo too. We all are.

"Maybe I will have that beer," she said.

"And maybe I'll have you," Candy said suggestively, handing Blue her half-empty bottle.

"Great," Blue said, her voice devoid of emotion. And as Candy went down on her knees in front of her and it began all over again, Blue put the bottle to her lips and drained it.

# A Night On the Town

"**D**rat," Kate mumbled, fumbling nervously with her bottom coat button. Some loose threads had got tangled around the button, and if she didn't take the time to unravel them, said button was going to come off, leaving a great, gaping hole for the wind to whistle through the minute she left the bar. "Damn," she swore again as the button responded to her impatient tugging by popping off and dropping to the floor.

That was what she got for refusing to do her darning, she thought, annoyed with herself. But then, it had been that kind of week: too much to do and not enough time to do it in. But never mind, she told herself; a lost button is not a portent of worse to come, it's just a lost button.

All day, as she had gone about her duties in the hospital, the idea had been growing in the back of her mind that she should go out to the bar. Certainly not to meet someone, since she was by no means ready for that. Just to be there alone, to rediscover some of her deepest roots, to sit quietly and smell the distinct aroma of a lesbian bar, to let the music envelop her, to observe, to renew a sense of kinship with other lesbians. She needed to establish an equilibrium, to feel the normality of it all. Maxine had taken away her trust in women, had destroyed her belief that it was possible to love and be loved in return, a belief which had already been shaky after her previous lover had left her for a man.

"You've just had a string of bad luck," Oats had said, trying to give her strength and to put the best face on what had been a disastrous relationship. But bad luck or not, she had no desire to tempt fate by trying again so soon.

"Lose a button?"

Kate looked up from her inspection of the grimy, littered floor and nodded.

"Want some help finding it?"

"No, I think I'll give it up for lost," Kate replied, taking her coat off and handing it to the coat-check woman.

"That's too bad. Those are nice buttons," the stranger said with a sympathetic smile.

"Oh well, I can always replace them all," Kate said politely, putting a dollar in the wicker basket on the counter and walking away. Women! Always on the prowl. Still, it was nice to know that she still had the ability to provoke interest.

Stop that, she told herself, sitting down at a table just inside the door. You're not looking, so stop thinking about other women. She ordered a mineral water and looked around.

There weren't many women in l'Entr'acte, but it was still early, just after eight-thirty. It would be packed by eleven, but Kate planned to leave before then. She hated crowds, especially in this boxy, airless, low-ceilinged bar, and although she was no longer afraid of her, she didn't particularly want to run into Maxine, who would undoubtedly be making the rounds of the bars on a Friday night. Unless she already had a new girlfriend. Kate didn't care to think closely about that; it inevitably made her wonder whether Maxine's next girlfriend was going to meet the same fate she had. That possibility made her feel guilty. But what could she have done? Call the police, lay a complaint and hope that Maxine ended up behind bars? Or that she would be forced to go for counselling? No, it wouldn't have worked. The police would have laughed her out of town or refused to believe her, and her private life would still have been invaded, ridiculed, dirtied. And what if by some miraculous chance she had been believed? How could she stand up in court and testify to her lesbianism? What about her job? Her parents? The resulting notoriety?

"May I join you?"

Kate knew it was the woman who had approached her in the coat check room, but she looked up anyway. "I'm not really in the mood for company," she replied, trying to let her down gently.

"I don't mind. I just don't feel like being alone," the woman replied frankly.

But Kate did. Frustrated, she frowned as the woman pulled out a chair and sat down. She stared at the dance floor, watching two willowy young women try to interpret a New Age song. They were not particularly graceful, but in all probability only a ballet dancer would have been capable of successfully choreographing music like that.

"My name is Gretchen," said the woman, holding out her hand.

"Kate."

"My relationship just ended, so I feel a little shaky," Gretchen explained.

"Mine too," Kate found herself saying.

"So we have something in common, then," Gretchen said, smiling.

Not really, Kate thought, looking at Gretchen. Her face was old, her body large. She seemed comfortable in it, her broad shoulders accentuated by the tailored shirt she wore. But what was Kate doing, staring at her like that? Gretchen was going to get the wrong idea. Kate turned away, but not before she saw Gretchen's smile grow wider, deepening the lines on her face.

"I wish they'd play some decent music," Gretchen said, ordering an orange juice from the passing waitress.

"Yes."

"It's not like the old days, when there was always something good to dance to," Gretchen added.

"I know."

Kate could feel Gretchen staring at her and wished she would stop. Perhaps she should leave; it might be the only way to rid herself of this woman, who had obviously decided to attach herself to Kate for the evening.

"Are you still in love with her?" Gretchen asked.

What impertinence! Had she no manners? And then Kate laughed at herself. She should know better; there were no limits in the bar. The only rules were those you made for yourself, for your own benefit. And everyone was fair game, everyone. She took a drink and said, "no."

"So you were the one who broke it off?"

"Yes," Kate replied calmly, refusing to think about Maxine. She would impersonalize it, sanitize it, remove violence from the equation.

"I wasn't," Gretchen told her. "I fought tooth and nail to keep her, but she wouldn't stay."

"I'm sorry," Kate said, and found that she actually was.

"After twenty years she just up and announced one morning that she was tired of me," Gretchen continued, sipping her orange juice.

Twenty years!

"I told her I would change, do whatever she wanted me to, but she said she was bored," Gretchen added. "Imagine that. Bored."

"I guess that can happen," Kate replied.

"But I wasn't bored, I still loved her like crazy," Gretchen said. "And I still do."

"I'm sorry," Kate said again. An old, eminently danceable tune rocked the jukebox, and suddenly she didn't want to sit there and listen to Gretchen pour out her heart. She hadn't the fortitude to experience someone else's pain, and she certainly didn't possess the energy to spend the evening comforting this grievously wounded woman. "I'm going to dance," she announced, getting up from her chair.

"I'll come with you," Gretchen said, rising eagerly.

And that was how, several songs later, she found herself tightly ensconced in Gretchen's arms, doing an old-fashioned waltz to an interminably long number. We must look like two old fools, Kate thought, praying that none of her friends would walk in and catch her in the act. This would teach her to watch her step when she was alone in the bar!

"Oh, good, another one," Gretchen exclaimed, her firm grasp preventing Kate from escaping.

"I'm a bit tired," Kate said, pulling back.

"Just one more," Gretchen coerced, not that Kate had much choice. Gretchen stood ramrod straight, her large, pointy breasts pressing into Kate's chest, her thick thighs virtually trembling with anticipation.

What now, a rumba? Kate followed Gretchen around the floor, feeling herself growing short of breath, although Gretchen showed no sign of flagging.

"This is wonderful!" Gretchen exclaimed.

It was certainly something, Kate thought, although she wasn't sure that wonderful was the right word to use to describe it.

"I could dance all night!" Gretchen said.

Oh, no!

"But I am thirsty," she added.

Thank goodness!

Kate followed her back to their table and finished her mineral water. "I have to go," she said, putting her empty glass down.

"But we dance so well together," Gretchen protested, rising from her chair.

"It was very nice to meet you, Gretchen, but — "

"And I thought you might like to spend the night with me," Gretchen said, her expression intense.

That stopped Kate in her tracks. All she had wanted was to spend an innocent evening in the bar, and here she had been propositioned before it was even ten o'clock! "Gretchen, I don't think — "

"Please. Sit down."

Kate sat and then wondered why she had.

"I know this is a bit forward, but I find myself quite attracted to you," Gretchen said brightly.

"Well, thank you very much, but — "

"And I'm very clean," she said earnestly.

Clean? Oh. Did she mean that she had dusted her apartment and changed her sheets or was she referring to something else, to one of those horrid venereal diseases that fed on sex?

"Gretchen, I — "

"It might be nice, Kate. Think about it," Gretchen added, resting her case.

Kate stared at her, her mouth opening with amazement, not at Gretchen's forwardness but at her response to it, because she actually *was* thinking about it! She had never been cruised so persistently and yet so gently in her whole life. Or so strangely. Was she attracted to Gretchen? She hadn't been repulsed when they were dancing, although she had been so preoccupied with following Gretchen and moving her feet in time to the music that she hadn't had time to react to the proximity of their bodies.

"I — "

"It wouldn't commit you," Gretchen rushed to assure her. "I'm certainly not prepared to rush into anything, but Kate, I'm lonely."

Ah. The truth of the matter. And there it was. Bereft of her long-term relationship, Gretchen was daunted by solitary evenings, haunted by the suddenly enormous family bed and the poignantly vacant chair at the breakfast table. Kate found that she could easily relate to that.

"And I think you're lonely too," Gretchen added. "So why shouldn't we enjoy each other while we have the opportunity?"

The most pressing question of a whole generation of lesbians. But at least Gretchen was being honest. No adolescent groping on the dance floor, no obviously false professions of love, no promises of a pie-in-the-sky future together. No, it was here we are together tonight, two mature people who have suffered at the hands of others, two women looking for comfort and perhaps sexual release without the need to play games.

"Does any of that make any sense, or am I being an old fool?" Gretchen said, and then she laughed.

Gretchen's ability to laugh at herself pushed Kate over the edge. "Yes, it does, and no, you aren't."

"Good. I was beginning to wonder," Gretchen responded.

Kate laughed. "If there's any old fool here, it's probably me."

"You?" Gretchen protested. "A young thing like you?"

"Well, I am nearly fifty," Kate replied.

"And I'm sixty-five," Gretchen told her.

"That's a nice age," Kate said.

"Well, it's an age, anyway," Gretchen replied dryly. "Now, have you had enough time to think it over?"

"Yes. And it's yes," Kate said firmly, meeting Gretchen's eyes.

"Wonderful. I'm sure you won't be disappointed," Gretchen said calmly, although Kate could see from her expression that she was pleased.

And Kate wasn't disappointed. Considering that she hadn't made love with a woman in nearly a year, considering that Maxine had so recently hurt her both emotionally and physically, it amazed Kate that being with Gretchen was so comfortable and that making love with her seemed so easy. Kate undressed with Gretchen intently watching, and then lay down with her on top of the plush, gold bedspread. She loved Gretchen's large, heavy breasts; she could have buried herself between them and stayed there forever, feeling Gretchen breathe, listening to the steady beat of her heart. But once the intimate dance of love had started, it took on a life of its own, a life grounded in their rising passion. Gretchen was inventive, talkative, whispering vivid comments in Kate's ear while she gently touched her, which Kate found terribly arousing. She came easily, and Gretchen was there throughout, holding her, urging her higher, and then following her. And incredibly, less than half an hour later it started all over again, their snuggling kindling desire and leading to a slower, even more tender exchange. After that Kate lost track because it simply didn't matter; this was undoubtedly the best sex she had ever had in her life.

Kate woke early, lying still in the darkness, listening to Gretchen snore. The bed smelled sweetly of sex, flooding her mind with fond images of their lovemaking. It was such a stroke of luck that she had possessed the good sense to override her natural inclination to automatically reject Gretchen. How long had it been since she had slept with someone on the first date? Twenty years? Not that last night had even been a date, not by the furthest stretch of anyone's imagination, she thought wryly. Talk about a fast worker!

"Good morning," Gretchen said, turning to kiss her.

"Good morning," Kate replied, and then it happened all over again, and she didn't care that she was going to be late for work. Very late. In fact, for quite some time she thought she might not get there at all, but it was just past lunchtime when she drove her car into the parking lot, feeling conspicuous in yesterday's clothes.

Gretchen had sent her off to shower while she prepared brunch, and then the two of them had hungrily devoured enough food for an army.

"That was good," Gretchen had said, the twinkle in her eye making it evident that she was clearly referring to more than the orange juice, scrambled eggs, wholewheat toast and pot of strong coffee.

"Excellent," Kate had added nonchalantly, pouring another cup.

"I meant what I said last night, you know," Gretchen had said, growing serious.

"I know," Kate had replied, her voice even. And she did. It had been wonderful, but that didn't mean they had to pretend they were in love. There were no strings attached, nor did she want any.

"That's even better," Gretchen had responded.

Kate had smiled then.

"Friends?" Gretchen had ventured, a look of uncertainty straining her face.

"Friends," Kate had replied firmly, and it was true. They would be friends, they would perhaps from time to time be lovers, but one would not get in the way of the other.

"A new friend," Kate murmured to herself as she rode the elevator to her floor, oblivious to the curious stares of the other passengers. So much better than a passionate affair. And safer, she thought, getting off on 6D to make a belated start on her day, hoping the head nurse was in the mood to be placated. Much safer.

There would be no possessiveness, no jealous scenes, no need to explain her private ruminations unless she wanted to. She was certain of this even though she didn't know Gretchen. It was clear that rather than try to start a new life by falling in love, Gretchen preferred to incorporate new people into her old life, to befriend women who would accept the status quo and not ask for more. Nothing could be more perfect for Kate.

She walked down the corridor, smiling at the nurses and patients she passed and humming the tune of the waltz she and Gretchen had danced to the night before. She felt happy, and she was darn well going to enjoy it.

# Friendship

Every year spring seemed to arrive in Montreal overnight, while people were sleeping, surprising the city's winter-weary inhabitants, although they should have remembered how it was from years past. One morning the snow was gone, right down to the last grimy centimetre, as if it had been mysteriously carted away in the night. Tender, green shoots of grass tentatively tested the warm air, and crocuses sprang from the sodden earth in otherwise barren front gardens. The winter's collection of dog droppings cluttered the busy sidewalks, and pedestrians were forced to step smartly to avoid the encroaching cyclists, who multiplied like rabbits with each warm day. People opened their windows and dared to hope, calling forth long-repressed memories of sunshine, heat waves, barbecues in the back yard, the fireworks competition over the river, the jazz festival, vacations in rented, lakeside cottages in the Eastern Townships or the Laurentiens.

Oats closed the door behind her and appreciatively sniffed the early evening air, wondering if other cities smelled like this on the first real day of spring. Whether it was a good smell or a bad smell she couldn't really say; it was just familiar, and a harbinger of better weather to come. Car exhaust fumes still not dissipated from rush hour, the muddy smell of wet earth, the too sweet musk of rotting garbage, the distinctive odour of dry heat escaping from the pavement, the fresh aroma of new plant life and of the barely perceptible buds sprouting on tree branches, garlicky hints of tonight's fare at the neighbourhood's abundant supply of ethnic restaurants, all these combined to form an unmistakable bouquet which she thought just might be Montreal's alone.

"Summer's coming," she said to Melba, hurrying down the steps to catch up with her.

"Doesn't it always?" Melba replied, slipping her arm through Oats'.

"This year I wasn't sure," Oats said half-seriously, earning a sympathetic look from her lover.

"I hope they're on time — I hate it when everyone is late," Melba fussed.

"I know," Oats responded complacently. Somebody had to worry about things like that, and if Melba wanted to, that was fine with Oats. She matched her stride to Melba's, working the stiffness out of her muscles. It was good to finally be back at work. Her boss had thoughtfully given her easy jobs, knowing that it would take time for her to recover her strength and get back into the hectic rhythm of the print shop, to remember and overcome the idiosyncrasies of each piece of equipment. Soon she would have some money in her pocket, although Melba didn't seem to care that she had been paying more than her fair share of the rent and groceries. She hadn't held it over Oats either, not like some women would.

The Greek restaurant on Prince Arthur Street was crowded, but their table was ready.

"I knew we would be the first ones here," Melba said plaintively.

"Look on the bright side of it — we get first choice on where to sit," Oats replied.

"Well, sit beside me, then," Melba suggested. "Who else did you say was coming?"

"Kate, of course," Oats told her. "And, get this: she asked if she could bring someone."

"No!" Melba exclaimed. "What, already?"

"Kate said she was just a friend," Oats added.

"Oh sure, tell me another one," Melba snorted.

"Yeah. Especially since she wouldn't say anything thing about her," Oats said with relish. "Not even when I practically begged."

"A-ha! A mystery woman!" Melba exclaimed with a laugh. "So who else did you invite?"

"Well, Kate said she wouldn't mind seeing Jo," Oats replied. "So I called her, and she's bringing her girlfriend too."

"All couples," Melba mused.

"I never thought I'd see the day," Oats declared. "The next thing you know we'll be moving out to suburbia and suddenly we'll be too busy mowing lawns, cleaning swimming pools and walking our dogs to drive all the way into town just to go to the bar."

"It sounds like you've got it all planned," Melba laughed.

"Are you kidding? Do you want me to die of boredom?" Oats retorted.

"Who's dying of boredom? And why? Are we late?" Kate asked, bending to kiss Oats and then Melba on both cheeks. "Isn't this fun? Just like old times!"

"Old as in last winter?" Oats joked. "Here, sit next to me."

"It seems like at least a decade since we did something as ordinary as eat out together," Kate commented. "Anyway, let me introduce you to my friend Gretchen."

Oats stifled a grin at Kate's emphasis on the word friend and slid out of her chair to shake hands with a tall, hefty, older woman, liking her immediately. Her handshake was firm, her smile real, her eyes clear, interested, without artifice. A nice, ordinary woman.

"Kate's told me so much about you," Gretchen said, releasing Oats' hand.

"Been spreading vicious rumours again, have you?" Oats quipped at Kate, who was chatting quietly with Melba.

"What do you mean, again? Always, sweetie, always," Kate retorted smartly, and they all laughed.

"My press secretary," Oats said jokingly to Gretchen. "Without her, I'd be just an ordinary dyke."

"Don't press your luck," Kate said with mock anger. "Oh, there's Jo."

"That shy little thing is her lover?" Oats whispered to Kate. "They look young enough to be my children!"

"Don't look now, Sue, but they *are* young enough to be your children; you're getting old," Kate replied as she turned to greet Jo and Jock. "Does everybody know each other here? No? Well, this is my friend Jo, and her partner Jock."

Getting old. Cripes. Maybe suburbia wasn't so far off after all. "Are you sure you're legal?" Oats snapped at Jock as she shook her hand.

"Sue!" Melba scolded. "Watch your tongue."

"And are you young enough to cut the mustard any more?" Jock snapped back even though her face had reddened.

Everyone roared with laughter, including Oats, who managed to sputter, "Have some respect for your elders," before she signalled defeat by returning to her chair and sitting down. "I'm starved," she said, picking up the menu.

"What else is new?" Kate asked, giving her a gentle hug.

"Well, you would be too if you had to eat what Melba feeds me," Oats grumbled.

"You've turned her into a vegetarian, have you?" Kate asked.

"I have my ways, but I'm not a miracle worker," Melba replied, making Kate laugh. "Should we order some wine?"

"Not for me thanks," Kate said.

"Anyone else?"

"Me neither — I'm an alcoholic, but don't let that stop anyone else," Gretchen said casually.

Kate looked across the table at her and smiled.

Oats would eat her hat if the two of them weren't lovers. Just look at the way they were staring at each other! That little devil! Where on earth had they met? Gretchen was no spring chicken, either; she was over sixty if she was a day. Of course that was a dumb thing to think; Oats was closing in on fifty herself, and sex had never been better. Maybe it keeps on improving until the day you drop dead. Now there was a thought.

"Sue? A glass of wine?" Melba asked.

"No," Oats replied slowly. She had been drinking too much before her heart attack, so why start up again? Anyway, she hadn't missed it after the first few weeks. "But I'll have a cigarette for dessert," she added with a grin.

"Like hell you will," Melba grumbled.

Oats watched Jock grimace at Jo and silently pocket her cigarette pack. "Do you two want some wine?"

"A beer, maybe," Jock responded.

"Make that two," Jo said.

Oats scanned the menu and settled on chicken brochettes. She folded the menu across her plate and turned and nudged Kate in the ribs with her elbow. "So tell your mother confessor all about it, Katey, me girl."

"She's a friend," Kate replied, studying her menu.

"Friend, hell," Oats scoffed. "Don't try to put one by me, sweetheart, because you can't. You never could."

Kate sighed and closed her menu. "All right. We met at the bar last week."

"You went to the bar by yourself? Holy shit!" Oats said appreciatively.

"Watch your language, mother confessor," Kate chided her. "Anyway, we sort of got together."

"Details, my girl, details! Otherwise how can I decide your penance?"

"Don't hold your breath, Oats. Anyway, like I told you over the phone, we're just good friends. I like her a lot, but that's as far as it goes," Kate explained. "Her lover of twenty years left her, and you know what happened to me. Neither of us is ready for the affair of the century, that's for sure."

"How's the sex?" Oats asked.

"Just fine, thank you," Kate replied, smiling smugly.

"I'm glad," Oats replied, touched. It had been so long. "Your penance is to be happy and sin some more," Oats whispered in Kate's ear, giving her a kiss on the cheek.

"Thank you," Kate responded. "Now dry up and let me decide what to eat."

The waiter delivered a bottle of mineral water, and two beers for Jo and Jock.

"A toast!" Oats cried, lifting her glass of mineral water.

"Yes, a toast!" Kate echoed.

"To the end of this bloody winter," Oats said, standing.

"To the end of winter," Melba repeated, rising and touching her glass to Oats'.

"To the end of winter," Gretchen said, smiling across the table at Kate.

"And to friendship," Kate said softly, blowing them all a kiss.

"Yes, to friendship," Oats agreed, taking a long drink. She looked around the table and sudden tears threatened to spill from her eyes. She sat down and blew her nose. "I must be getting old and sentimental."

"No, Sue, you're just getting better," Melba replied, squeezing her hand.

The older the better, like ripening cheese or aging wine? Well, Oats supposed that suited her fine, especially since she couldn't do anything to stop it. Not that she would even it was possible, she decided. She liked herself this way. For the first time in her life she was content with what she had. She no longer felt like running off in every direction searching for something elusive and unattainable. Relationships were not automatically perfect, and wishing couldn't make them so. It took interest, motivation and work.

"I love you," she whispered to Melba.

"I know," Melba replied. "And I'm glad."

Oats blew her nose again, and then the food came. They talked, ate, debated whether to let Jock smoke over coffee and decided they would if she begged, and finally strolled off to the bar and danced the warm, spring night away.

# *Also from gynergy books*

*By Word of Mouth: Lesbians Write the Erotic, Lee Fleming (ed.).* " ... contains plenty of sexy good writing and furthers the desperately needed honest discussion of what we mean by 'erotic' and by 'lesbian'." SINISTER WISDOM **ISBN 0-921881-06-1 $10.95/ $12.95 US**

*Each Small Step: Breaking the Chains of Abuse and Addiction, Marilyn MacKinnon (ed.).* This groundbreaking anthology contains narratives by women recovering from the traumas of childhood sexual abuse and alcohol and chemical dependency. **ISBN 0-921881-17-7 $10.95**

*Fascination and Other Bar Stories, Jackie Manthorne.* These are satisfying stories of the rituals of seduction and sexuality. "A funny and hot collection from the smoky heart of the Montreal bar beat." SINISTER WISDOM **ISBN 0-921881-16-9 $9.95**

*Friends I Never Knew, Tanya Lester.* In this finely crafted novel, Tara exiles herself on a Greek island to write about five extraordinary women she has met from her years in the women's movement. In the process, Tara unexpectedly writes her own story. **ISBN 0-921881-18-5 $10.95**

*A House Not Her Own: Stories from Beirut, Emily Nasrallah.* "For centuries we've been seeing war through men's eyes. Nasrallah's unflinching yet compassionate prose presents it through the eyes of women." BOOKS IN CANADA **ISBN 0-921881-19-3 $12.95**

*Imprinting Our Image: An International Anthology by Women with Disabilities, Diane Driedger and Susan Gray (eds.).* "In this global tour de force, 30 writers from 17 countries provide dramatic insight into a wide range of issues germane to both the women's and disability rights movements." DISABLED PEOPLES' INTERNATIONAL **ISBN 0-921881-22-3 $12.95**

*Lesbians Ignited, Carolyn Gammon.* This impassioned first book of poetry delves into the fiery heart of lesbian life and love. "Gammon's work is a positive representation and celebration of female sexuality." WLW JOURNAL **ISBN 0-921881-21-5 $9.95**

***Miss Autobody, Les Folles Alliées.*** In this celebrated and hilarious play, the women of Anytown, led by a savvy group of feminist mechanics, thwart a scheme to show porn videos at a local bar. *Miss Autobody* depicts the effects of pornography and misogyny, and splits your sides in the process. **ISBN 0-921881-25-8  $10.95/ $9.95 US**

***The Montreal Massacre, Marie Chalouh and Louise Malette (eds.).*** Feminist letters, essays, and poems examine the misogyny inherent in the mass murder of fourteen women at Ecole Polytechnique in Montreal, Quebec on December 6, 1989. **ISBN 0-921881-14-2  $12.95**

***Triad Moon, Gillean Chase.*** Meet Lila, Brook and Helen, three women whose bonds of love take them beyond conventional relationships. *Triad Moon* is an exhilarating read that skilfully explores past and present lives, survival from incest, and healing. **ISBN 0-921881-28-2   $9.95**

***Woman in the Rock, Claudia Gahlinger.*** A haunting collection of stories about forgetting and remembering incest by an award-winning writer. Gahlinger's characters live near the sea and find consolation in fishing, an act that allows for the eventual, triumphant emergence of the "woman in the rock." **ISBN 0-921881-26-6  $10.95/ $9.95 US**

***Where Once Our Mothers Stood We Stand: Women's Suffrage in Newfoundland, 1890-1925, Margot I. Duley.*** In this important and lively book, the rich history of the women's suffrage movement in Newfoundland is uncovered. Duley draws on diverse sources and includes fascinating interviews with descendants and friends of the suffragists. **ISBN 0-921881-24-X $12.95**

***gynergy books*** is distributed in Canada by General Publishing, by InBook in the U.S. and in the U.K. by Turnaround. Individual orders can be sent, prepaid, to: ***gynergy books***, P.O. Box 2023, Charlottetown, PEI, Canada, C1A 7N7. Please add postage and handling ($2.00 for the first book and .75 for each additional book) to your order. Canadian residents add 7% GST to the total amount. GST registration number R104383120.